Rachel was born to June and Terry towards the end of the year in 1968. Living in Staffordshire, then Wolverhampton, and attending at first, local schools before going to an all-girls school. Rachel wrote short stories at school, keen to share with particular teaching staff, but did not get the response she wanted. Her ambition to write grew stronger from this time. Now a wife and mother to two beautiful children, she finds the time to keep that writing passion going.

To my children Paige and Joshua for believing in Mom, and my husband Stuart for just being him.

Rachel Leadbetter

SHORT STORIES

Nourishment and
the Uninvited

AUSTIN MACAULEY PUBLISHERS™
LONDON • CAMBRIDGE • NEW YORK • SHARJAH

A CIP catalogue record for this title is available from the British Library.

ISBN 9781528922708 (Paperback)
ISBN 9781528963886 (ePub e-book)

www.austinmacauley.com

First Published 2022
Austin Macauley Publishers Ltd®
1 Canada Square
Canary Wharf
London
E14 5AA

Author's Note

Thank you for choosing to read my short story, I feel extremely honoured. I do hope it meets your expectations of an interesting read. Enjoy!

I always knew that I wanted to do this. So, being able to transport it from rough prose to text in readiness for someone to critique is very exciting indeed. I have discussed ideas and short stories with people at school when I was younger and did not get the feedback or support I craved. This did not stop me from writing; however, it did prevent me from sharing. A teacher once said to me, "Why would you feel the need to mention such personal things in a story like going to the toilet?" My answer was, "This is a natural action and makes the story more realistic." She did not agree and was quite challenging and derogatory about my story writing. I would imagine that now, she's dead; possibly because of alcohol overuse and nastiness of soul!

I found it amazing and satisfying, yet invasive watching people read my work. Just as a vampire has to be invited into a house; my readers also had to have an invite because my fear of being judged was so great. One of my fears is that people will see me differently after knowing what I am capable of expressing and that, could taint me as people are opinionated.

I was never afraid of failure but I very much sought praise.

I always felt different from others around me as I was not particularly girly with straight bobbed hair and thin legs like some of the popular girls and I never had as many exciting things to talk about as they did. I also did not pile on makeup (actually did not know how, but they did not know that). I was very much the loner with my thoughts and feelings and carried almost a tonne of emotional baggage. Hence, where I feel I carved out my ideas using the thoughts and feelings, I did my utmost to keep hidden. Hidden they were but I embedded them deep until I was able to put pen to paper.

Would I do things differently if I got the chance? Hell yes! I would go into certain situations with a mature response and attitude and disclose stuff that I felt at the time should be kept hidden. I have gone from victim in a few situations to holder of the secrets, which in retrospect, should have been spoken about. I didn't want to hurt my friend, hence, my reason for keeping quiet. This same friend who sat with a group singing stupid, horrible songs about me and taking the mickey. This same friend who was a complete slag and smelt of mould, whose uncle was a kiddy fiddler and parents were alcoholics. I took the abuse from the girls, and I smiled and laughed along with it. A holiday abroad, in a cherry emblazoned bikini, approached by a strange man who felt it right to caress my body… I remember telling Mum and Dad this but I can't remember their reaction. This certainly did not affect me at the time but later on in life, I feel that it did. As an actress, I survived; as a strong young woman, I conquered. Feeling trapped and not knowing who I was, I became the real me in my stories. I became the unbeatable, strong-minded, kind, caring theatrical person I felt I was.

This person really is me and I can now see my strengths and realise what I went through, was a lesson in life and hardships. I won – if there is indeed a purpose of being the victor, I feel, I won every day and gained the experience to fight another.

Sometimes life can be difficult when we try to fit in with people from different lifestyles and we attempt to rediscover ourselves in the hope that the person we uncover will face acceptance. I have very few regrets now, from early life just the one where I held myself back until the age of 48, to realise my worth.

I dedicate this short story to my husband and my children who are all very much alive and well.

Joshua and Paige, please remember Mummy loves you when you read this. I will always be here for you and never be afraid. A mistake is a lesson to learn from, a loss is a realisation of something you cared for dearly, an acknowledgement of knowing that emotion. A drama is an event that you conquer with style and a win is a perfection at its best.

Embrace all the emotions as life brings it all like a box of fruit, what you do with the fruit is your choice.

Love, your perfect Mummy. xx

2014

The end – mostly known as the finale, complete, no more but for me, this was the start of a beautiful future, a life I wanted, no, needed. In fact, deserved!

My new mantra is, life is for living, no regrets and no worries. Don't live in the past, only in the future. Along with a new start comes new people, new faces, new beginnings, new lives.

Eat well, drink well, be happy. Fulfil yourself with happiness.

Now is present, functional, and existing. Do not throw chances away of true happiness. You never know what is around the corner.

Here today, gone tomorrow, and all of that rubbish. Talking of rubbish that is now mostly recycled, so here today, gone tomorrow, back again in another form! Oh, such is life.

Life quotes:

"Isn't it funny, how day by day, nothing changes but when you look back."

– C S Lewis

"Do not judge my story by the chapter you walked in on."

– Unknown livelifehappy.com

"You should never regret anything in life. If it's good, it's wonderful. If it's bad, it's experience."

– Unknown

Nourishment

Chapter One

Smiling weakly at the flaxen-haired, strikingly good-looking policeman, I got up and strode into the kitchen to wash up. I was doing everything like a machine, no feelings, no emotions no energy. Just getting the task in hand completed, was the only thought that crossed my mind. I started to fill the bowl with water and asked my guest if he would like some coffee to wash down the meal. He readily agreed and I finished the washing up and set to putting the coffee pot on using my regular smooth coffee granules, which tasted quite like cinnamon and rich. It is at this point, as I switched the machine on and the obligatory gurgle of the coffee maker began its journey to complete its set mission, that I crumbled into tears.

I felt the tears stinging my eyes and my cheeks became inflamed with hurt, anger, and embarrassment as I shook uncontrollably. Detective Constable Brevan McGinn tentatively touched my shoulder and I suddenly became silent as he caressed my fingers with his fingertips, giving me a sense of comfort and warmth when I thought all was lost. I began to feel protected from my thoughts before he decided that a sharp exit would be the best decision, as he was getting too emotionally involved with me.

He gently touched my hair as he turned me around by my shoulders and gazed into my wet eyes, which were red with pain. He kissed the end of my nose and whispered that he would come over tomorrow evening, after his shift. I gave him a weary smile and followed him to the door like a mewing pussy cat, silently pleading him to stay with me. I knew it was killing him to stay in control of his feelings as it was for myself, filling up with mixed emotions, ones I couldn't, at this point, show on my face let alone put into words.

As I watched him walk down the path to his car, I felt lonely again. It was nice having him around especially at a time when I was searching for comfort and solace. His long legs striding down the path signalled power and protection. With every step he took, being so purposeful and driven, he was an asset to have around. He turned to wave before he drove off and I felt myself go giddy with excitement and nervous energy, quickly being replaced with hurt and sadness as I re-entered the house. I missed him already. Sadness filled my whole body, giving me a paralytic feeling as I became one with myself, and had to face the next few hours alone, completely alone.

As Gerard's wife, I was the first person to be investigated over his disappearance. For a murder charge to be brought, the prosecution must produce what the Law calls '*corpus delicti*', Latin for 'body of the crime'. No body, no evidence, no murder weapon.

All I'd left from my wonderful, devoted husband was a note.

Miriam,

I have to go out, see you later for tea.

Love you,

Gerard xx

I gave the note to the police twenty-four hours after he failed to return home, where his devoted and loving family was waiting for him. I asked them not to destroy it in any way, as this was all I'd and the children had left; one measly, pathetic piece of paper with the fresh ink from his pen, scrawled on it so perfectly. I'd fight back tears of pain and intense misery. Each droplet seeming harder and harder, resisting the temptation of just letting go.

I was in charge now and I felt unbelievably deserted. Helpless. Useless. Powerless. My children needed a strong loving mother to help them come through this situation until Daddy came home. How do I tell them that I don't know when he'll come back or where he is? How can I place that negativity on them? I can't make them grieve more at their immense loss.

Our children are intelligent and pragmatic with their approach to life, always being able to deal with situations with no dream-like intensity, only relying on the facts. They put this approach into everyday life and schooling. Thus, they appear centred and content. We approached this situation as you would a mathematical equation. We looked at the situation and made decisions from there.

When the facts come out and we establish exactly where Daddy is and what he's trying to do and return, we can then support each other, to help us move forward. However, currently, all we are aware of is, that Daddy's not home, after leaving a note. This is worrying as it's well out of character. Daddy always came home. He often left us love notes but he always came home.

I've held both my children close to me at different times following Gerard's absence and we have talked about why he's gone. Many theories have been suggested from the children, such as; he had an affair and he's gone to get married and have another family; he was shot and buried somewhere on one of his hunting trips; he's gone to join a religious commune and forgotten us, or he's being held hostage somewhere. The hostage idea, I felt, was the most exciting but also, the most unbelievable but who knew.

I don't like the other woman slash family idea and said Daddy would never leave us for someone else. However, I was fresh out of ideas as to what had actually happened to him. I did, however, always impress positive thoughts onto the children and along with the help and support from our amazing friends and family. I tried not to speak negatively about him in any way, even though, as the grieving widow, I was very angry at his departure.

Any moments of intense sadness, I exercised on my own, away from the children and anyone else. This was my way of remaining strong in front of people, and not giving in to emotions as I saw that as a failure. I didn't want my children to have to comfort their mummy. That wasn't right, not right at all.

New information was always well received and we kept up our hopes that one day, Daddy would return to us all. Both sets of grandparents were supportive, and regular visitors, and wore the pain of the absence quite heavily on their faces. Although, in front of the children they were strong and positive, loving and fun which is what they needed to have more of at a time like this.

Bed in Summer.
In winter, I get up at night,
And dress by yellow candlelight.
In summer, quite the other way,
I have to go to bed by day.
I have to go to bed and see
The birds still hopping on the tree,
Or hear the grown-up peoples feet
Still going past me in the street.
And does it not seem hard to you,
When all the sky is clear and blue,
And I should like so much to play,
To have to go to bed by day?

A Child's Garden Of Verses by R L Stevenson.

My children did go to bed earlier some nights; most nights. I couldn't stand the constant questioning and the inevitable upset. How do I explain a loss, what do I say and what answer do I give? My head hurts working out new scenarios and trying to remain positive in the face of adversity. Adversity had emotional consequences, affecting the mental health and well-being of my babies.

While my head was exploring its scenarios, I chatted to my nearest and dearest, divulging my innermost fears and keeping a lid on what I could knowingly share with my children. I felt myself going mad! I was jealous of my children as they could show their emotions and crumble in despair. I had to be the strong one and hide how I felt. Life gets to me at times, it's total unfairness, all of it.

I put myself in a world of hurt – I felt my devoted husband had left me for a younger, prettier model and this, I shared with some close friends only. I know they would discuss me eventually with other friends and word would get about it. By then, I would be stronger and would cope with it, I was sure. As the kitchen got hot, I would be warned and be able to cope with the intensity, knowing I had some support from my friends. In times of despair, you find out exactly who your real friends are.

The Land of Story Books
At evening, when the lamp is lit,
Around the fire my parents sit;
They sit at home and talk and sing,
And do not play at anything.
Now, with my little gun, I crawl
All in the dark along the wall,
And follow 'round the forest track
Away behind the sofa back.
There, in the night, where none can spy,
All in my hunter's camp I lie,
And play at books that I have read
Till it is time to go to bed.
These are the hills, these are the woods,
These are my starry solitudes;
And there the river by whose brink
The roaring lion comes to drink.
I see the others far away
As if in firelit camp they lay,
And I, like to be an Indian scout,
Around their party prowled about.

So, when my nurse comes in for me,
Home I return across the sea,
And go to bed with backward looks
At my dear land of storybooks.

A Child's Garden Of Verses by R L Stevenson.

Chapter Two

It all began, I think, when I was a child, an only child at. Born to wealthy parents and never having to want for anything, I was on the easy street in every way possible. I was privately educated in all areas of the curriculum and I excelled at everything, much to the pride of my parents. If I struggled in anything academic, we paid for private tuition and lessons and I then succeeded. Success was the ultimate end goal and showed achievement and power. Gone was the idea that 'try, try and try again' works, when I can pay someone to teach me correctly in the first place, and check that I can retain the information and adapt it to the given situation.

We lived in a five bedroomed detached house with three reception rooms and four bathrooms, two suites. A large kitchen and dining room with an L-shaped conservatory added to the glamorous abode. We had a long driveway leading up to the house and were flanked on both sides with a high fence and walls of greenery. We had an impressive water feature that was tall and fell through three levels to the final basin underneath which was elevated off the floor. This held fish, some of the most colourful ones I had ever seen, and large well-fed fish. In contrast to this, we had an amazing pond out the back, with super koi inhabiting it, with other pond life all existing in the same water utopia.

This led to a bridge that had to be crossed to enter the rest of the garden and the summer house. I used to imagine that I lived in this water world, where I had my little underwater paradise with other amphibious creatures. It was an escape from everything else I felt and faced, and I imagined my own little stories and events always being rescued by the energetic, keen-to impress-gardener.

It was picturesque and gave an impression of perfection which would say if the garden looked like this, the house must be phenomenal. The picture-perfect family in the picture-perfect home. We certainly had an impressive home and my parents employed workers to keep it maintained. They worked around the clock (the workers, not my parents)

I never had any real need to get a job and I always fell on my feet, whatever risks I took. I know this must sound great to someone who has to struggle through life to make ends meet but to me, I didn't feel fortunate, I felt robbed. I was bored of my life, from when I got up to when I went to bed. Bored, bored, bored. I didn't feel spoilt or ruined but I did feel trapped.

It's this exact feeling of boredom that spurred me on to find some excitement as my good fortune was my ultimate undoing. Therefore, if I was to place the blame, of course, it would be my parents' fault all the way.

Mr David Bordeaux and Mrs Hannah Bordeaux, previously Camille – the couple with everything; the couple who were so lucky to have met and made it work and be so successful. Both of them originating from lucky backgrounds, where their parents worked hard to establish themselves in the communities. Not short of a penny but at least they worked for the majority of their fortune. Two well-known families with high standing morals, collaborating to become one.

My parents were typical showy people with an almost sickening desire to make themselves appear normal. My father, the owner of his company, was forever making new deals, buying and selling shares. His office was big enough to hold a party in and he had his own bathroom. His staff was young and pretty, always super polite trying to impress him at all costs. There was a large turnover of close office staff and I always felt that it was odd that the supply of young, flattering, eager-to-please, pencil-shaped office staff, was always high. Each one of them must have fitted particular criteria such as long legs, ample cleavage showing, the ability to wear high-heeled shoes and not fall over, always smiley and apply makeup well, and not forgetting to creep-up well to the boss and understand the word 'no' doesn't exist. I was always jealous of his overzealous attention towards them. When I was around, they would fall over themselves to speak to me and make me feel welcome. They would try so hard that it was embarrassing. Father would always look so admiringly at them, trying to engage with me.

My father was a strong-featured, good-looking type of man who oozed power in his daily makeup. He was the type of man who expected people to do as he said and for the most part, people just did. He was likable too but I felt that people were, sometimes, afraid of him. This didn't just run in the workplace but at home and with friends too. He was a tall, handsome charmer, able to sell ice to the Eskimos. He was Mr Popular and it appeared that people didn't really want to piss him off. He was a man's man and a boy's favourite but there was always a line, which even his friends, dared not cross. Father had this element of red mist, where his anger became so visible, it was like a shroud, suffocating his victim, creating an unbreathable atmosphere and leaving a feeling of unwelcomeness, loneliness, and despair. Disappointment became an unhealthy and unwelcome feeling to those unfortunate enough to be on the receiving end of Father's wrath and it was, at all costs to be avoided.

My mother met him during an evening of entertainment between the families and as if by magic, they got on well. My mother was very popular with friends of both sexes and was a fantastic host when her parents put on dinner parties. She oozed prettiness and was particularly feminine in her attire and personality. She was polite, gracious and her etiquette was to die for. Well known in the community as an established young woman in her own right and would be consulted by all ages regarding issues like catering, functions, interior design, and relationships. She was seen as the young lady with everything, so when she married my father, she became the woman everyone wanted to be, the Oracle, the Peacekeeper. The Lady of the Manor. My mother was the supreme It Girl! Whatever you dreamed of becoming in later life, the It Girl would have a feature in there somewhere and a period of obsessiveness, carving out part of your life or how you led it.

Mother always wore her slightly curly blonde hair up either in a bun or a clip, grasping all the stray ends and allowing them to curl around each other, suspended on her head. I feel that her hair along with her figure were the biggest and the most noticeable assets. She was known for her ladylike look and demure presentation. She would be annoyed if Father grabbed her to hug her and it wasn't already choreographed and he had caught her hair. If some of it came down out of the clip, it was a drama and a half, and she would have to excuse herself to put it right immediately.

Maybe in retrospect, that's why they only had me. I really could not imagine my mother doing much to get her hair ruffled. Obviously, they managed to copulate but then I do wonder, *how did she give birth?* Maybe paid for me to be extracted with the least discomfort to her, and then a tummy tuck and liposuction to follow immediately afterward, with the hairdresser at her side throughout along with a make-up lady! Bless my mother! How glamorous she always was. The kind of glamour that comes with money well spent and manufactured products, previously tested and explored on willing subjects with fabulous proven results. The glamour industry certainly profited for a while with Mother's input. That was until she decided to tap into it, releasing her brand of make-up and glamour products. Wow, she was certainly a hard act to follow in many respects.

Apparently, I was bottle-fed, (from what I hear from the Nursey (the paid help) and Nanny) as if I could expect anything close to motherly contact. I was a good baby, hardly cried, and wasn't bothered if I was in a full nappy or not. I was in a bed at an early age and in my own room. My doting Grandparents told me that I was a credit to my parents and I was a keen and fast learner but independent and self-controlled. I went to bed at the set times and took pride in my room and my immediate area. I did what I was told and always glowed with obvious pride whenever my grandparents praised me.

They were forever telling people how amazing I was and strangely enough, I don't remember hearing this from my parents until much later on in life. And many an evening would go by with stories and adventures, and I would go to sleep and relive everyone, especially those with a gruesome act in them. I remember asking my mother once if all stories end happily and she told me,

"We all make our happiness. Happiness can be created, dear, and we have control of our destiny and how people may view us." I always found this a little odd and wondered exactly what she meant by it. Maybe in later years, I would find out.

I have disjointed memories of my youth, but fond ones, mostly with my Grandparents. I can remember beach days and sandcastles and fun with my Grandparents, with my parents collecting me after they had completed their dinner parties or work, etc. I cooked loads and had fantastic times outdoors with horses and farm animals. I had a few friends over at my Grandparents and we always did the picnic thing with some form of entertainment. Life was good. I had few challenges and even the few hills I had to climb, were easy enough. I did what I had to do, what was expected and I exceeded all others' expectations with style, always achieving what was set out for me. My grandmother would often say, "They're cut from the same cloth. You're so like your mother."

I guess, in some ways I was, but in some ways, I was extremely different, I feel.

Of course, my parents wanted the best for me and they cared in their own way but they were never tactile or loving, physically. The hugs and kisses were very rare and if they ever did take place, they felt horridly uncomfortable, practically alien. They were always there for me though and would do or give me anything but sometimes, their demands got too much.

It got annoying having to attend particular functions and dress up nicely to impress, always be the lady, the daughter of the esteemed family. To say and do the right thing in the correct manner. The woman, my friends would be envious of and wish their lives were like mine.

My mother would spend time doing my hair and trying to encourage me to take further pride in myself and my 'feminine appearance'. I did like this, as I felt we bonded in this light and we shared precious mommy-daughter times. It was at these times that I really felt accepted by my mother and her feeling proud of me. She would look at me, almost seeming like she was jealous as if she wanted to be me and relive parts of her youth. I often wondered if she was really happy and if, what I witnessed as her daughter, was real or fake utopia. If it was real, this is what I craved for. If it was utopia, it was bloody awesome too! A bite of that cake, I definitely wouldn't refuse.

I had boyfriends who would have hot dinners. I was slim, blond, and had bright blue eyes, which was once described by one such conquest as endless pools of ocean blue which you could fall into (and he did!). My hair was naturally curly and hung carelessly down my sides coming to my waist. It would be longer once I straightened it but that was rare, as it took too much time and effort. I used to tie a flimsy piece of ribbon or soft cloth around the middle, just to control the Rapunzel-type hair. I wore limited makeup but when I did, I made an effort to over accentuate the blue of my eyes and used rich reds for my lips (as advised by my mother whose perfect facial features were accentuated by simple yet effective makeup contours). It does have to be said that she was perfection personified and how she gained her knowledge of makeup and hairstyles, I would possibly never know; she was a lady full of useful knowledge and a master in the art of keeping those around her happy. My beautiful mother. A wonder of nature's gifts and all of her adoring followers.

As far as boys went, Mother took a back seat and welcomed every boy into the house, knowing their presence in my life would be very short-lived. She would say 'another friend darling' and would make an effort to get to know all of them, just to satisfy her curiosity. If she knew the families, she would never let on but was always dutifully polite and pleasant. There would always be fresh cake and scones with tea and coffee available, almost seeming like it was on tap. I had no idea how Mother did all of these things, and I could imagine her being up during the night, baking with her hair a mess, and her makeup all smudged. It's probably at these times that she would really be herself and not the painted doll she alluded to. The doll, that always fitted the shelf right and posed correctly for her adoring followers. I remember feeling awesomeness, a kind of admirability towards her, almost like I felt, I had to please her, acquiesce at times, and be a part of her entourage. Almost like I had backstage tickets to a phenomenal show. She was the perfect host and the perfect mother. Of course, we had staff that did particular jobs and I imagine, they would've prepared food such as freshly baked to order but they always seemed to be scarce or barely there. In fact, almost not there. What the eye couldn't see, the mouth could not critique. I like to use this term. It has a great effect on my day-to-day life.

After showering my guests with food and beverages, she would become instantly busy with her new business ventures and bustle away in style, to work. My boyfriends would often comment on how beautiful and striking my mother was and this would strangely chill me, as I would, sometimes, see it as competition. She was indeed gracefully good eye material and again, I wondered how happy she really was.

I can admit now, years later, that I admired my mother to an extent, that I would love to emulate her. At least the surface of her, the part she portrayed to everyone else outside of the family as I was yet to really see and understand the person within, the real woman herself.

My father had little to do with any of my friends and I felt, he just thought or hoped, I would grow out of it. If he saw any of my friends, he'd always say hello and then make himself scarce. He was way too busy making money, doing deals, and looking impressively sleek and rich, that was my opinion anyway. He had his fingers in many pies, creating new deals and opportunities, extending workplaces, and encouraging higher sales. He was known as an entrepreneur in some fields, a magic man spreading positivity through business opportunities everywhere. He could turn his hand to anything and appeared to be a paid advisor too, with links in court and legal arenas, in almost every country.

My parents mixed in particular circles and had already found some promising dates for me, which they would mention, every now and then. I knew, eventually, if I didn't manage to find my own perfect choice of man, my parents would step in. I always felt that they were laughing to some extent, seeing me with all of my little friends and watching how things progressed, then come crashing down. I often wondered, did they enjoy my failures, gain some gratification from them, some sadistic joint pleasure, which they would then turn around in conversation with me, to make me feel like I'd let them down. I felt that I needed someone in my life, but I wasn't sure of who that should be. I wanted to have a perfect partner-cum-friend like what my parents appeared to have with each other. I wasn't sure how I would maintain a long-lasting relationship with the same person for a particular length of time. How is the excitement of a new relationship maintained when it is not new anymore; how do you sustain normality which in effect is what takes place after newness; how do I please my parents; or maybe I should be saying how do I impress my parents, never mind, meet all of their surreal expectations?

No wonder I was so tired of life, confused with emotions, drained of energy, bored with normality, seeing the buzz but identifying the wrongness of it as it would not live up to the expectations of my parents. Yes, my parents were definitely to blame for my wrongdoings.

It's right what the people say, it's always the parents!

I mixed with many different people and as long as I was out when my parents hosted evenings, they were not too fussed about who I went with or why. Our perfect family picture remained that way, picture-perfect.

Then along came Gerard. He had great charisma, walked with a purpose, and was able to socialise with everybody and anybody and asked for nothing in return. He had it all, seriously good-looking, with blond-mousy hair, slightly wavy which he wore scattily draped around his face. He was tall and thickset with a chiselled jawline and handsome looks. He was admired by both sexes, everywhere he went. His eyes were deep brown and he sported long lashes, quite uncommon for a guy. I would be fighting for his attention when we went out, and it always amazed me when men would approach him and ask him if he was single! Gerard took it well, always smiling and teasingly pleasant whilst he dashed all hopes for his potential admirers.

Gerard's parents were extremely wealthy and influential in their community with a big business shared with Gerard, enabling him to be set on the map and regarded under the family business in his own right. He was just starting to branch out on his own, extending the already very large existing company. He had amassed quite a fortune from all the potential clients and had already found suitable new wealthy interests worthy of a piece of his knowledge and a possible slice of the businesses. The job itself took Gerard away at times and he would always make a fuss of me before he left and come home armed with gifts on his return.

Gerard was the perfect catch for anyone and my parents set about planning our future and I do have to say, they made a good choice. Gerard was besotted with me from the start and I was happy to go along with it. He was a good person and he spoilt me rotten. He had to chase me quite a bit initially, as I was held back, wanting to see how much he was interested in me before I would appease him with a return of affection. He doted on me and I, in turn, found myself pretty much hoodwinked by his constant charms.

I was very much wrapped up in his world and wanted to please him, constantly. I knew what he liked and how to please him and I concentrated on making an effort when I knew he was around. I wore the perfume he liked and the short skirts, he grew fond of, with killer heels. I began to do my hair in ringlets and styles, which I knew, turned him on. My makeup was sexy and feminine but minimalistic during the day. At night it was to suit the evening and type of event. I knew him inside out and back to front, I knew how to please and tease him and always played the shy, embarrassed type, just as I knew he would want me to. Though at times, I played the dominatrix if I felt it was warranted. Gerard was a little wary of me at these times, as he preferred to be in total control and I played my cards carefully, to please and also get my satisfaction to a point.

Throughout all this time, I was acting out a play, where I was very much in control of his feelings, libido, life, etc. He just didn't know it but I certainly did, and this gave me overwhelming power and made me feel complete.

I put this down to always feeling out of control with my parents and being told what to do. Always fitting the bill, playing the part of being the perfect daughter. Now I was to be the perfect wife, be as expected, do what is expected, say what is expected. Underneath this façade, I was in complete control and played the game of life like chess pieces placing them in order of moves, to gain complete control but seemingly doing what others expected of me. Over time, I became adept with the checkmate moves and played with more false sincerity, becoming seemingly more convincing and always having a backup plan.

To my willing crowd, I was helpful, honest, genuine, and earnestly kind; the real me was objective, manipulative, and all moves considered before carrying them out with the result predetermined. Each move was calculated and I often moved into checkmate sooner than was required, developing a tricky situation needing to be teased back to normality. This provided unbridled energy, teasing with excitement and tension always providing its own foreplay.

I felt like I had all the power, and Gerard was my puppet, just as my parents were and all my previous boyfriends. Even when I ended relationships, I always maintained a strong unacceptable bond with all past loves and held their hearts and feelings in the palm of my hand. Even when they moved on to new loves, I was always their main focus, quick stolen thoughts which led to a secret phone call, and frantic and desperate fondling, mostly ending up with sex. They would then often disclose, their hidden love and how they felt they could never move on without me. In every instance, I became the pussy cat, chasing the mouse and when I had it in my claws, I dangled their life precariously, asking them to take risks to prove they really loved me. I developed a fin fugal alliance within all my many conquests. Hence, creating a further obsession, a reason for them to want to stay around.

The power of having someone's reasoning in your hands was immense. I could literally change decisions and chosen paths and it was careless fun on my part but harrowing and distressful of the other chess player.

A couple of them took their lives after I had led them into false insecurities and made them so depravedly satisfied that they felt they could only continue to live if they were by my side. I had had to tell them I could not give them the continued unrequited love, which they craved, and, if they proved themselves by taking their lives, I would know they genuinely loved me. This is when I would then promise, we could continue into the afterlife regardless of all around us and be happy forever and ever.

I didn't feel selfish, just loved and a necessary part of these people's lives. A part that they desired, needed and obsessed over for their pure selfish gratifications. I helped them have a purpose see a light experience some happiness. I actually regarded myself as an angel at times.

An angel! I tore families apart, took fathers away from their children, left wives widowed! How funny am I? LOL, I can always see a positive in the worst of situations. Bless my Sox!

I am actually not that bad, I remember everyone fondly. Those people that take their life or die for me, I treasure the memories of them. They were very brave in the end, so in love with the person they thought I was and that is sweet, very sweet. I do hope, that in death, they found some satisfaction and relief, and possibly a nympho angel who could please and tease up in the clouds. They didn't really die for me and I was no murderer. I didn't hold the knife or pull the trigger. I merely put the thought in their head and the mere suggestion of meeting me in another life, where we could be together forever was enough to push them over the edge. The promise of me whether in life or death was the big prize. There was no proof of my involvement in their lives. They were careful as they didn't want their new partners or family and friends knowing about our times together. That was one of the deals they had to agree to, that they could spend some quality time with me, keeping our trysts secret and maintaining the special contact, and keeping the excitement alive.

Some men are really stupid, especially those with their brains in their genitals but hey Ho, back to the story.

Gerard.

Gerard and I got married and three children later, I felt that I had reached my ultimate goal. My glass was always full, and they were gold-rimmed glasses that I wore every day. As I looked into the eyes of my children; Joey 12, Maverick 10, and Chloe 8, I could see little miniature versions of Gerard and myself. I never felt so proud. I'm a mother, a housewife, and my husband, a self-made businessman, and a very successful one at that. My children are so happy, clever, and well-behaved. They want for nothing, but they have an understanding of achievement and how it is up to them to succeed but that as parents we will always support. I hugged them every day, told them I loved them at least twice a day, minimum. I made sure that I was what I would consider being the perfect parent. I watched them play, helped them play, supported them in homework projects and activities. I was always there for them and advised and praised them continuously. I chose fabulous friends for them and made sure that I got to know the parents. I helped out at school activities and any fetes etc. I was always available for them, the perfect mother.

Gerard was the perfect father; played with the children when he was home, changed nappies, and was a complete hands-on dad. He was more relaxed about bedtimes and routines than I was, but he was a fun-packed parent. He was attentive with all of them and only his study was off-limits when he worked from home.

My parents were very different with my children. Whether it was something to do with the grandparent title and being able to hand them back, I didn't know, but they were full-on and attentive. I have to say, this affected me greatly and I was at first very much disturbed with this but again I hid my true feelings and smiled graciously as was taught as a child. I never can remember being hugged by my father or mother, even at my wedding, my hand was held, and my hair stroked and that was an emotional moment. However, throughout my children's young lives, I watched my parents dote every precious minute on them, playing with them, hugging, cuddling, and kissing them goodbye. I occasionally thought that I saw a possible look in their eyes, of regret, at how cold they had been with me, but I feel this is possibly wishful thinking on my part.

My relationship did not change with my parents. It remained the same just in adult form. Although, when my children were mixing with us all, it became easier to communicate as the atmosphere was more relaxed and no one had to impress each other and be the better person. We were quite silly and daft, and these were fun times that I will always remember with fondness.

A lot of friends adjourned our social calendar; friends in high and useful places. We were friends with two high court judges, solicitors, lawyers, and a few members of her local majesty's constabulary. We had various functions and celebrations and I was always the willing host to our influential guests and their partners and wives. We were well known in the area for community events, charity raising, and awards evenings. Our children would always be around us, playing their parts in our wonderful lives, showing how well behaved they are, and I invited both grandparents on both sides to all of the functions.

Gerard's parents were amazingly fun with the children and adored them. They would have them at a minute's notice and do anything for them. They always took them out places and introduced them to their friends with pride and love in their hearts. Our children are extremely blessed, indeed.

We are a wonderful family with an extended tight and supportive network around us. Our friends' children played with our children. All activities were well-attended and monitored for appropriateness. After all, we had to play the game well. Our children are happy with affection shown readily by all family members. Rounded, happy, well-achieving; everything we could've ever wanted for them.

I know we were seen as the golden couple and as the king and queen of Dartford shire. We had taken over our parents in this role and we made sure we did it well. Our love had no bounds; we were always happy and always supportive of others. I cooked for the locals and I have to admit, being famous for my homemade meat pies, casseroles, and cakes was empowering. Our children got on with everyone and attended the local school where Gerard was a parent governor and I volunteered for fun days, picnics and school shows, etc.

I started a service for the homeless and I took my children to the community kitchens. We all helped to cook, so at certain times a month, three meals were available for people in need. This gradually increased as more folk decided to help out, voluntarily, and soon, we were providing three meals a week and bed and breakfast. We had someone from the council come and help with supporting work-based ideas and training. This was so successful that we began to branch out in other counties using our success as a tool to measure for other schemes. We called ourselves the Angel Service, as of course, all of us working these shifts are angels.

Gerard had regular men days and even some nights, he would go shooting and bring the game home. I didn't like it to start with as I was always sad about the death. He assured me the animals did not suffer and provided a service. He showed me how to prepare it, but always preferred to do it himself. He described it as the final act of the experience.

He'd put the animal where it belonged in a kitchen recipe. He was an experienced gunman and a proud hunter. He didn't believe that the animal should suffer any more than it had to. He was a clean shot too. I joined him on occasions, and I was envious of his calculating and control before the shot rang out to signal the life being extinguished from the chosen prey. I couldn't bring myself to take an active part, but I was happy to watch. Gerard loved this about me. I was always a bit goofy with blood and not able to handle death well. He liked to be the big strong protector. It suited us, and Gerard was always the decision-maker and the instigator. It was just our way.

We adored each other and everyone. We were a team to be admired and envious, all in one go, and we wore our hearts on our sleeves.

Then, boredom set in, and everything changed big time.

Chapter Three

I realised that I was bored. I was pulling out all the stops to act like a willing and devoted wife, even more so that Gerard would not suspect there was anything wrong. Changes needed to be made and I wanted out. I didn't know what I wanted but I couldn't remain in this picture-perfect existence. I was admired by everyone we knew, all wanting a piece of our lives, but I felt I was struggling to continue. I was playing a part in a show, and I was losing the plot somehow. I wanted to be in the wings sometimes so I could shake off the mask I wore and just be me. The tension was unbearable at times.

Sex was always amazing, and Gerard was very good between the sheets. He always made me feel special and I was hugely turned on, but it became very same. I played the part well in the bedroom but at times, I had to fake the lot rather than just the end game. I noticed Gerard had become especially close to one of our friends, Susan, and I was jealous to a point of distraction. I watched them both together imagining them being hot and steamy, and it being a huge secret. I gave them opportunities to fulfil their desires by leaving them alone on many occasions, but I never caught them doing anything inappropriate. In fact, one time, I realised that they had organised a party for me as a big surprise and that's what they were discussing. The party was amazing and the gifts were priceless. They had together achieved a phenomenal event and I was overwhelmed by their kindness and generosity, even though I knew they were possibly sleeping together! I felt guilt at having had the wrong thoughts but then dismissed them as my interpretations of their strange actions together. From that moment on I did feel like Gerard was with someone else and I imagined it to be deeper than just a one-night stand.

My dark thoughts continued, and I realised I wanted a new man and a new life.

I had a real passion; it was reading but I was choosey about what I read. It had to be thrilling, a little gory, dark, and dangerous. Total fantasy but ridiculously exciting. I kept a variety of novels, all in paperback, on shelves and I regularly dusted them, being careful of the covers. I read my books holding the covers apart, just enough so I could access the print but not to permanently bend the cover back. That way, the books remained new and not old and tatty. I didn't appreciate worn-looking books and I obsessed over who had read them before they came into my hands.

I read up on old serial killers who had gotten away with murder sprees for a while before being caught. This real-life shit got to me. They actually did this stuff and they were famous for doing it! Of course, they were caught the majority of them anyway. But what made someone a killer? There is a lot of neuroscience and moral juggling behind the decision to take a life. The human brain is coded for compassion and guilt; a type of empathic pain that results in the person inflicting harm to feel a degree of suffering that can be sometimes as intense as the pain the victim is enduring.

Psychologists and criminologists will examine the evidence for years to try to attempt why people do certain things. I feel it's down to the individual.

Some people kill for money such as assassins and hitmen. Some for jealousy bordering on obsessiveness, some for power, and some, I believe, are accidental deaths. Deaths where fun and power went too far, resulting in the inevitable but with unwanted results at that time. I read about people who had had such awful childhoods, experiencing traumas and abuse quite unimaginable that helped pave their way into serial killers.

Theodore Robert Bundy known as Ted was an American serial killer, rapist, burglar, kidnapper, necrophile, and paedophile operating in the 1970s. He was responsible for over thirty victims, however, the police felt there were more. Ted only confessed to thirty. He was married and led a normal life.

He once called himself 'the most cold-hearted son of a bitch you will ever meet'.

Polly Nelson, a member of his defence team, said: "Ted, was the very definition of heartless evil."

I liked Ted. He was intelligent and kept himself out of the electric chair for a while with his ingenuity and knowledge of criminal law, which he used to his advantage. Ted used his gentle persona and soft tones to convince his victims that he needed help and was so grateful. At home, he was the quiet husband and he only slipped up due to his sexual tendencies where he had asked his wife to play dead while they had sex. He wasn't careful enough!

John Wayne Gracey was also an American serial killer and rapist. He was responsible for the deaths of at least thirty-three teenage boys around 1972, by assault and torture. His idea of disposing remains was his eventual undoing, as the smell of the rotten carcases under his house alerted services. He was likeable, affable, charming, and widely respected in his community. He was easy to get along with and everyone loved and admired him.

Some of John's quotes were eye-openers:

"I should never have been convicted of anything more serious than running a cemetery without a licence."

"The dead won't bother you, it's the living you have to worry about."

"A clown can get away with murder."

"I don't remember killing anyone. I could have done it without knowing it. I am not sure if I did it."

John spent 14 years on death row in California before he was executed by lethal injection in 1994.

He was a funny man. He had his clown side, had his way into the public's hearts where he gained trust and new friends, and his sadistic side where he engaged in homosexual activity which had to be forced to satisfy his needs. I liked John and I admired his way of manipulating the people around him, not only his family and friends but the community; the general public. He was phenomenal.

John Hague murdered his victims and disposed of the remains in a vat of acid. He had a life of strictness regarding religion in which all manners of casual entertainment were prohibited; from carnivals to musical shows and reading of magazines. He was an extremely bright child but governed by rigid routines and rules (I likened this to my rather strict upbringing and not being able to let the animal loose, living a lie). In 1949, he burst into the headlines for the murder of

41

many victims, dissolving the remains in acid. He was called a vampire because he used to drink some of the blood of his victims. (Gerard always said he would say a silent prayer for the animal before he shot it, thanking it for its unknowing sacrificial offering). John was responsible for approximately six to nine deaths, around 1944. He was an English man and battered or shot his victims to death. He sold the victims' possessions and collected substantial amounts of money. He was executed by hanging in 1949, Wandsworth prison.

The absence of the bodies meant there was no case, so no evidence. However, evidence was sufficient as bloodstains were found on the walls, victims' jewellery, as well as a gall stone in the sludge in the yard, and a set of dentures from Mrs Durand-Deacon, sealing his fate.

Circumstantial evidence and forensic evidence are prominent in such convictions. Other people are called upon to discuss the case and assumptions are made based on what evidence there is.

I read that a body can be completely dissolved in about a month. The important factor was the heat generated by the interaction of acid and the water present in a fully hydrated human body. This would have to be in some sort of tank and big enough to fit a corpse inside.

I would need a steel tank, concentrated sulphuric acid, and protective clothing. I couldn't just purchase these items. It had to be planned out and obtained through different means over a while.

The tank, I acquired from a friend who worked in a meat processing plant, and I pinched some overalls on the way out. The acid, I obtained over some time from different suppliers, using an alias. This whole process took over three years of careful planning. Over this period, I could feel a rumble of excitement generating which threatened to overspill and leak everywhere. The act of keeping it contained was a sexual thrill and I generated this energy into our lovemaking which was always accepted with readiness from a willing and loving Gerard. Our sex life became so exciting that Gerard started to get suspicious, saying that he would stay out a night or two. When he came back, it would be fabulous lovemaking as I missed him so much. He was so God damn adorable!

Every time I collected my delivery of acid under my many aliases such as Joanna Hague, Julia Guahe, Jemima Aughe, etc, it always made me laugh as no one questioned me and I was always in different personas with wigs and transport. Sometimes the thrill was just too much and a couple of times, after I was driving back, I had to pull over and release my sexual tension in any way I could. The third time was the last out in the open as I was disturbed by a hitchhiker who was just passing through and caught me in the undergrowth just about to climax. I was very embarrassed and wary until he dropped on the floor beside me to show me his toolbox and said he wasn't stopping in town. I made him promise to move on after our encounter and completely drained him of energy and juice. We howled loud and scratched each other every time we climaxed and when we lay there, looking at each other, we just started again until both of us were sore and bleeding with friction but glowing with relief.

I thought, maybe I just missed the thrill of someone new and the open spaces with the constant threat of being disturbed but it didn't make a difference. I assaulted several willing victims over the next few months, each one found on the roads from the plant, each one just passing through. The only difference was that I wasn't caught pleasuring myself, but I was caught trying to start my vehicle which started pretty fine after I had been to pleasure county, and back a few times. This was new for me, and I enjoyed the power and control of the fact that no man ever felt intimidated or scared.

Only one of my stranger encounters decided to not leave imminently and I had to take measures to ensure it did happen. Strangely enough, it was a lady called Madeleine who was as risky and as false as me. I had met my match and we met up a few more times following our first encounter. She said she was leaving to start a new life in Vegas and would wait for me. I gave her false addresses and numbers and encouraged her to wait for me in Vegas promising her the world and its oyster. We had our final meal in a restaurant on the outskirts of town where we enjoyed pasta and fine meats in rich sauces topped with hard cheese and strong red wine. We spent the better part of the night together and I left during the early hours to go home.

Gerard was at my parents' with the children and would be back about 10 a.m. so I wanted to be home and showered, and all evidence of my lady experience washed away. As much as it had been strangely satisfying it left an uncomfortable feeling with me and I had to disperse it as soon as possible. Later that day, I heard on the local news that a lady passing through the town had had a fatal accident in her jeep where the brakes had failed, and she had turned the vehicle over exploding into flames. It was later discovered that the brakes had been tampered with and the fuel line had been cut slowly, pouring gasoline around the vehicle, this being the main fuel of the fire which burned the lady to death.

I'm sure she suffered, and I felt cheated as she hadn't fallen for me in the same way as previous conquests. Her suffering was pointless and non-gratifying for me, and I felt that she managed to get one up over me. Maybe women are too sharp and emotionally stronger or maybe, I was the better actor and she felt she had me on a string much like a tampon. Only the string is only so long and the weight of the cotton wool when sodden would be more likely to drop out, thus breaking the bond.

Again, in my world of complete depravity, I was the winner.

Gerard and I had a wine cellar that he was renovating. He left me in complete control of it and behind a false wall, I hid all of my supplies. In front of this wall was a huge rack full of wine which I was trying to place in alphabetic order and colour code it. I involved Gerard in the planning of the wine racks and shelves, and we accumulated a large selection of different wines as we had recently purchased a vineyard in France. This maintained our regular supply of innocuous liquid. We shared our wine amongst all our grateful guests, and we discussed the colour and texture of each one, analysing it for future reference. We became quite the wine connoisseurs, and we often sent our visitors down to the cellar to refresh supplies. This, of course, also reaffirmed to me how well the false wall and extra room were hidden. The only other factor would be the smell.

I had read that limestone would be a good agent to keep the air fresh and if necessary, mix with existing soil and rock as an aggregate. As a reagent in flu-gas desulfurization, it reacts with sulphur dioxide for air pollution control. This was used by John Wayne Gacy to help destroy the bodies of over thirty-three teenage boys between 1972 and 1978. The stench of rotten flesh was his downfall and I had thought of how to prevent that. The desiccated remains were found in the crawlspace under his home where he lived with his wife. Dismembered remains were found all underneath the property and in the surrounding river. He was as good as guilty, as ever he could be. In fact, some of his victims have yet to be discovered.

If the smell was the offending factor, I decided the less there was to dispose of, the less chance of a putrid smell there would be. I decided to get myself equipped with a few tools for my experience and some limestone for good measure.

Throughout this time, I played the dutiful, loving, and loyal wife and the perfect mother. I became more compassionate, more loving, and caring and I doted on my husband. To all around us, I was the model for society to follow for the perfect family.

We even discussed having more children and we shared our thoughts with family members and friends who showed excitement and warmth to our ever-extending brood. I did think, at one time, I could be pregnant as the morning sickness was overpowering and I was struggling with similar stages of pregnancy I had experienced before at the start of each of my broods' existence. Thank God, it was a head experience and not a reality. The mind is a powerful thing, turning all possibilities into a mind-blowing subconscious of false reality. A time zone developed to encompass thoughts and wishes which are made tolerable by inactiveness; just existing in the back of the brain and continuing to fester possibilities.

Thank fuck for mind-blowing falseness!
Fake, falseness – how wonderfully silly is this? I am
suddenly reminded of a pointless poem;
'One fine night, in the middle of the day,
Two dead soldiers got up to fight.
Back-to-back, they faced each other
Drew their swords and shot each other.
A deaf policeman heard the noise.
And came and shot those two dead boys.
If you don't believe this poem is true
Ask the blind man he saw it too.'
Meaningless but funny shit! Like part of my life.

Chapter Four

One weekend, all three of our children stayed at our parents' house, taking it in turns at each visit. The children loved it and always returned a little more spoilt and loved up after each grandparent affection assault. I almost felt jealous of their ability to soak up the ever flowing attention and feel like the special little people which they are. I almost longed at times to be in their shoes and be a sponge to affection and attention as I always wanted to be. It was also innocent and exciting back then and stress was a million miles away.

Usually, at these times, when I had the house to myself, free of little monkeys, Gerard would go fishing or out with his mates from the rotary club and I would be able to do my spring cleaning and bake some meat and fish pies and cakes and fresh bread. Sometimes, when Gerard had been on the hunt, he would return with pheasant and rabbit and help dress it, showing me how to slice the meat from the bone and prepare for stews and casseroles. If I knew he was on the hunt, I would prepare pie cases of fresh pastry with a puff topping that rose gradually while baking.

On one such day, I prepared pie cases, casseroles, stews, and soups. I also did a lot of creamy mash potatoes and cheesy toppings to add to the dishes. The only ingredient I left out was the meat. I had decided to delete my husband's existence and I planned the erasure with complete synchronicity right down to the finer details. It was on Friday evening that I decided to complete the deed. Gerard returned from work, leaving the car on the drive, ready to put it in the garage later. He needed to pop over a friend's house within walking distance to collect some papers later, which loosely translated to him staying there for the better part of the evening and returning well after the children and I had retired to bed, slightly inebriated. Obviously, with all children at their grandparents', it was one last worry for me.

This was quite a regular occasion and I never objected. After all, I was the absolute perfect wife who loved and adored my partner and my children. To the outside world and Gerard, we were the perfect family. That night, Gerard's parents collected the children for the weekend, and off they went with overnight bags packed and oodles of fun to be had.

When Gerard entered the house, I ran up to greet him (as I always did) and gave him a kiss. The reaction was always the same; he reached down to my buttocks and gave them a sensual squeeze whilst nuzzling my neck. This usually pissed me off incredibly but seeing as I was planning his demise later, I decided to make the most of the impending fuck. He saw all the food in the kitchen and asked what was for tea, I told him I was the starter and I dragged him upstairs for a bath. This was as easy as could be, Gerard was desperate for sexual relief and nearly beat me up the stairs.

I had decided if I was going to extinguish his life then I deserved one last piece of marital pleasure. Gerard was as willing as ever and didn't disappoint. After an amazing session of mind-blowing lust and sex games, I enticed him into a warm soapy bath where I promised to abuse him till he cried out for mercy. As Gerard leant over to stir the bubbles, I hit him hard and square over the head with a frozen joint of pork that I had hidden under the sink, wrapped in a towel.

I hit him again and again and again until I had sweat so much, and his head looked kind of caved in like playdough on a model, that's fallen off a high table hard. The blood was everywhere, God, he had so much of the stuff. It was warm and sticky and smelt funny. The joint was quite heavy, but I had perfected my aim and gotten used to the weight. I knew if I got this wrong and Gerard survived, there would be hell to pay.

I don't think he felt anything he was too numb from the sex session, and I had crept upon him by surprise. In fact, I was fast, like lightning, like a superhero, like a frigging ninja; ninja wifey!

She's fast. She's incredible. She's the one you really should watch out for. She's the killer. She's the winner and she will take what she can get and more and more (sing this to the danger mouse tune, it's so funny).

Anyway, back to the story, I had a job to do.

I put the joint of meat in the oven and started to cook it. I used towels to start cleaning up the blood from the floor. I worked like a robot; using Gerard's chainsaw I separated his limbs from his torso. It was surprisingly easy, and I worked at a constant speed, being careful with the saw. Messily, I placed them in bags and began the arduous task of slicing meat from the bone. My friend was a butcher, and his talents came in very handy. I had sucked up to him in more ways than one to learn and copy his skills of the trade and God, all that sucking was worth it. I was a top slicer and filleted parts with ease.

How ironic was it that Gerard had also shown me how to skin and fillet and I had always shied away from it but secretly watched every detail. Bless my dismembered hubby!

I was surprised at how easy and malleable the flesh was and how it came away from the bone was a magnificent sight. It felt like art! It was such a shame I had to kill my husband to finally appreciate him and his art forms. The fat was all bobbly and yellow and was a funny consistency when separating it from the flesh. It made me feel a little nauseous. As I separated flesh from bone, muscle, and tendon, I was amazed at the amount of blood. The arterial blood was the most exquisite as it gushed and gushed with its mission to leave the existing vessel and cover me and the bathroom floor. It was so warm and so sticky but of a thickness, I can't describe. It reminded me of when Gerard returned home from hunting trips with his catch and how he had shown off his talents feeling as if he was impressing me. Poor, stupid, gullible Gerard, bless him.

Eventually, there was so much blood, splattered everywhere, I began to find it difficult to separate chopped flesh from fatty waste and chipped bone. The fatty parts were the worse to touch. There was so much of it too and I made a mental note to work out more to limit my fatty parts.

I switched on the shower and let a nice easy flow cover all the remains. I then methodically bagged the waste, almost working on auto pilot. The amount of stuff in the bathroom surrounding me was scary to a point that I stressed about being able to clean it all up and dispose of it. I knew my plan was well thought out and a lot of time had been taken to secure this event and make it successful. I had to sort the plug hole out a few times to remove excess debris and gristle, and I made sure to bag it all.

All the fatty flesh, useless tendons, and viscera went together in one bag. All the bones and Gerard's head (what was left of it) went into another. Feet, hands, and genitals went into a third bag. I took my time over this, amazed at how pathetic his manhood really was. How can something that fleshy do anything worthwhile? Thank God for foreplay.

I was very much aware of the time and everything I had left to do, and I continued with my task in peace, work-type of fashion. I had already removed Gerard's wedding band and he had taken his watch off before his bath. I also took out his hoops from his left ear and I kept them safe in an envelope until I could leave town on an errand where I would drop them down a drain.

All of the flesh, I knew I could use; I took downstairs to the kitchen. I filled two stock pots, three saucepans, and three casserole dishes. I added powder mix and onions to the casseroles and parsnips, carrots, onions, and leeks with plenty of herbs was added to stock pots. For the meat in the saucepans, I intended to drain off the liquid as it cooked and add a rich sauce to use as pie filling. I added my favourite ingredient, 'all-purpose seasoning', a spice so individual but salty and garlicky all in one.

The pungent smell of cooking meat filled the air; it was like chicken and pork with a hint of rabbit and a sweet peppery essence. The meat cooked surprisingly quickly, and I had to lower the heat, careful not to overcook it.

While everything was slowly cooking, I ran back upstairs to collect the bags. I carefully placed them in the vat of acid in the basement. This took many trips, but the wonderful smell of cooking meat spurred me on. The vat was quite full, and I carefully placed the lid on the top. I slid the false wall back into place and secured it. As I returned upstairs, I started to clean the carpet and wipe the floorboards with my steam cleaner. The bathroom was a mess, and it took a while to clean. My anger kept me in check, and I cleaned fast and furiously. God, Gerard was a dirty bastard, even in death, he bled out everywhere, useless fuck. Now that made me giggle! I had one last fuck and I cleaned him off the floor, how funny!

I used umpteen amounts of bleach and cleaning fluid and my steamer threatened to die on me. I lit candles everywhere like I usually do and there was no sign of anything untoward had taken place. Bleach removes all evidence of blood and hides the smell of death. The candles were of a deep aromatic nature and added to the generous smells of cooking in the kitchen but masked the bleach aroma beautifully.

When the cleaning was complete and the cooking underway, I sat down to assess the situation. I would fill the freezer with Gerard and of course, I had cooked the joint of pork mixing it with chopped buttock and base of spine flesh. I would fill the kitchen freezer and our two chest freezers and would label all pies and stews and casseroles as I usually did. Gerard had bought me the extra two chest freezers for when he came back with the game. He was full of good ideas and brainwaves and now he will see, personally, just how good they are for storing. A shame that he can't appreciate it.

I placed the cooked meat with stewed root veg in the casserole dishes and I spooned generous amounts of creamy mash over the top with a cheesy topping. I did the same with the pastry cases and the stew was looking lovely. I tasted bits and added more herbs as I cooked. In one of the dishes, I added passata and garlic. As I have a mincer, it was easy to do spaghetti Bolognese, and I did a few generous portions of that. It took me a while to get everything made and the counters were full of cooked dishes, in all shapes and sizes.

As everything cooled down I washed up the remainder of the dishes and put them away. I then cleaned the other bathrooms as thoroughly as I had cleaned the death scene. So, all smelt of bleach but all had lit candles in them, emanating a deep Italian musky smell which complimented the meat dish smells, once again.

Then the final part of the plan came into play. This was what I was worried about if I was to be totally honest. The rest was just acting out a play but this bit for me was real.

Once I had finished packing everything away, I took out the note Gerard had wrote me three weeks ago. I had placed it in a food bag to keep his fingerprints on it and not mine. I placed the paper on top of the television set. I left his car on the drive and his car keys in his jacket pocket, his house keys I conveniently lost in a storm drain.

The next day, I woke up and began cooking a variety of vegetables and defrosted a few pies. I invited our neighbours and friends over for a meal that night and I chilled a few dozen bottles of white and red wine. God, I loved to cook and entertain. Everyone was willing to oblige, and we sat down to tender pie seasoned to perfection with fluffy mash and roast potatoes, Yorkshire puddings, and bread sauce. The table was full of people and both reception rooms were buzzing with activity. Lots of people talking, eating, and generally, having a great time. They helped themselves to seconds and wine flowed lovingly from bottle to glass, bottle to glass.

My after-dinner treats were a feast not to be missed. I offered chocolate gateaux, strawberry cheesecake, raspberry pavlova, and deep-dish apple pie with custard which everyone enjoyed.

Early evening, I decided to state the obvious that I had not seen Gerard since last night, had anybody else seen him?

Together we called both sets of parents and all our friends to no avail. I showed everyone the note, the parting gesture from Gerard. Everyone was supportive and helped with enquiries, showing obvious concern and rallying around, empathising. People started to depart around 10.30 p.m. and those left, helped me stack the dishwashers and hand-wash some items. I left the glasses to drain naturally, and we discussed Gerard's absence. I was the concerned wife but not too worried as he had done this before, and I didn't want him returning and then gloating to his friends about how scared I had been and overreacted. My close friends agreed with me and advised me not to worry until the morning if I had still had no contact.

Sunday morning, I called the police with my parents and children at my side. I made an effort to keep everything as normal as possible so the children would not be affected but it was so hard. I told the children Daddy had gone away for a while and I hoped to see him soon.

We had to stay strong and support each other through this difficult time. We grieved together.

Chapter Five

My children's sadness tore at my heartstrings like a violin being violently plucked. I still felt my needs were far greater though, I had to be happy for them; I had to be happy and contented to be a good mother. Therefore, without question, my happiness and fulfilment was vital. I became the most significant person in my children's lives. No longer did they share their affections, this time I had it all to *me*.

Gerard was everywhere in the house, on the walls in photographs and his clothes still lying around the house like a dirty reminder of his existence and my guilt. His favourite chair still had his coat slung over the back of it as he had left it that fateful Friday.

I organised counselling for all three children, and they had to do wishes and feelings. They had lots of support from school and family members, and they got through the months supported and feeling listened to. They will adapt, they are my children. They are strong and resilient, and they are loved.

Each day that passed, I kept living the same way for the children and my parents. I co-operated with police fully and often had three or four officers over for dinner including the judges. Our friends were vigilant as they were constantly concerned for my welfare. Their company, I was most grateful for, and it was good for the kids.

Also, I loved to entertain.

It's now been three months since Gerard left us all. We have a very nice constable called Brevan, who we have known for a while helping us out, in more ways than one. He spends a lot of time at our house and eats with us constantly. He is good with the children and plays games and entertains them. He has a good job and is very successful and my parents rather like him. I feel they are trying to play matchmaker as they can see the positive effect he is having on us all. Plus, another positive, he is a complete horse under the covers and is not shy to try new things. We have experimented a lot, especially in the wine cellar. The thrill of climaxing by the wine skewered on a policeman with Gerard's remains dissolving behind the false wall is complete and utter heaven.

Life is starting to look good again. We always have meat in our freezer, and I have to admit Gerard tastes good, especially with a bottle of house red.

Money, large sums pending, three children and one grieving widow, desperate to keep family life on an even keel, desperate to try again with another partner, hopefully for longer this time around.

After all, I had tasted the sweetmeats of success. Gerard was a good husband, he always made sure we were looked after and well-fed.

Sometimes, when I am on my own, delirious with rich wine, I shake with excitement and complete disbelief which I manage to pass off for grief when in the company of others.

I, Miriam Gough, managed to not only kill my husband, Gerard but also successfully dispose of his remains. There was no case against me and I was fortunate to be a close friend of a detective constable who had had a huge thing for me for quite a while. I intended to find out exactly how huge this thing was and I'm sure I was in for a wonderfully fulfilling experience. Eventually, Gerard's financial assets would be freed, and I would be able to access them as and when I pleased. I mean, after all, he had just deserted his family! A wife and three children, all under the age of 13 years, he had left behind.

Oh sweet, seasoned life!

The Uninvited...

**"Is all that we see or seem
But a dream within a dream"
Edgar Allen Poe**

To my children, Joshua and Paige, whom I have full faith in, and I know will not turn out like me, willingly disappearing into the strange, horror, parallel universe that I call my sanctuary.

Rachel.

Just a thought…

Fear is an emotion that all people will experience at one time or another. It can be a simple scary feeling or a more pronounced fear such as a phobia manifesting deep within the subconscious, waiting to erupt at the least expected moment. One can fear the imaginary as well as the all too real. A person can also be neurotic with their suspicions and can gradually fear everything and everyone.

How can a person say what is good and what is evil?

Can a person be evil?

Could it be a dirty look, a nasty thought, or even is it possible to be possessed?

Can a building consisting of solid bricks and mortar inherit evil? Manifesting itself in the building blocks and gradually creeping up the walls, through the floors, and into the belly of the house itself.

Can old and gnarled trees be the spirits of once tortured innocents at someone else's depraved hands?

Just a thought.

Chapter One
Friends

Summer holidays! Schools out! Streets and parks are littered with children of all ages. Laughter, giggles, shouting and the shrill assertive call of overcautious mothers fill the air. The little town of Caine was at its liveliest. Shopkeepers were run ragged having to keep an eye on nimble-fingered adolescents and be subservient to women with children who felt the need for useless chit-chat. 10:30 a.m. on a Monday and the ice cream van was already a prominent feature. The weather was bright and warm, holding promise for the rest of the day.

The door knocked, I ran downstairs and opened it excitedly. Standing outside was a mousey, tousle-haired guy with a tanned face, muscular frame with broad shoulders all carried by long toned legs. He greeted me with a huge grin that appeared to spread from ear to ear. His name is Liam, my lovely friend, and confidant.

"Well, hello sexy," I greeted him.

"Hi, babes, got your glad rags on, ready for adventure?" Liam quizzed.

I looked him straight in the face. "For you, anything!"

Liam grinned and went over to open his jeep, as I did the routine of locking the house and putting the alarm on, as instructed by my wonderful parents. The phone started ringing just as I was closing the door, but I left it as Liam shouted, "Charlie, come on, we're going to be late!" and started the jeep to accentuate his urgency.

"I'm coming!" I shouted ignoring the phone and getting into the jeep.

The jeep smelt new and clean, and it was obvious Liam had made an effort to get this vehicle looking good for our road trip. It was also a very smooth drive and Liam was a calm driver, which for me, was a huge relief; always fighting travel sickness on any journey.

Our next stop was to pick up Edward and then onto Connie's where Damon and Christine were waiting too. We pulled up outside Edward's house and Liam honked the horn. A few seconds later Eddie appeared, looking slightly harassed. I had a secret thing for Eddie, so secret that I hadn't discussed it with anyone other than Connie, who was sworn to complete confidentiality. Eddie was about six foot, dark-haired, laughing eyes with long lashes, good bone structure, full lips, and always managed to look smart and clean. He carried an air of elegance, grace, and reservation that I found thrilling and inviting. He climbed into the jeep and favoured us with a smile and a sniffle.

"Still got that wretched cold?" asked Liam. "What you need is a good woman!"

"With this cold, I doubt any woman with half a brain would accommodate me," grunted Eddie.

The 'brainless' me looked out the window and smiled as I knew I would accommodate him. My thoughts were interrupted as the jeep suddenly stopped. We were outside Connie's house. This time, Liam got out of the vehicle and made his way, looking a little awkward towards the front door. He had a huge thing for Christine, and I could see why. She was slim, dark, and very attractive with olive coloured skin and large brown eyes. Her brother, Damon, was also good-looking, but he knew it. A classic flirt and pretentious at times but witty and prepared to be the butt of many jokes. He was never short of a girlfriend and appeared to not care if he had one or not. He was one of life's lucky people, where everything goes right.

Connie had blond hair, like me, except hers was straight cut into a short bob, shaved at the nape of her neck. Slim build but never showed it off as she preferred the tomboy image. Whilst Liam was greeting everyone and organising bags in the boot, I took my chance to chat with Eddie.

"Do you mind if I sit in the back with you? Only I'm sure, Liam would rather have Chris by him."

"If you can stand me sniffling then, of course, I don't mind." He smiled as I climbed into the back, rather too enthusiastically, but I didn't care.

"Are you looking forward to our little jaunt? You seem a bit down in the mouth at the moment," I asked, looking him straight in the face.

"I'm fine," he said, stroking my cheek grinning, "just want to make sure I get my pub lunch, that's all."

I found myself staring at him with a fixed admiring smile painted on my face. He giggled and got comfortable in his seat as Connie climbed in with everyone else.

"Well, here we all are and off we go along with sniffle here, so who's up for catching a cold?" She looked at me winking. The journey was full of sarcasm and wit, general chit-chat, catching up on school gossip and who is with who

65

conversations. Soon it turned to serious stuff like food and what we were thinking of having for dinner, etc. Damon and Chris handed the map between them discussing the route then passing on the information to Liam who drove as smoothly as ever.

We had decided on a few days away, stopping for bed and breakfast and having tea at local pubs. We passed through a few nice towns with their quaint little shops and houses. The weather was warm and by the time we reached the next town, passing by the sign saying, 'Welcome to Serenity', we were desperate to stretch our legs.

Liam pulled up just outside a pub called 'Serene Pasture'. This was aptly named as the building backed onto a farm and there were fields to the one side and behind, full of lush grass and beautiful flowers, picture-perfect.

I was the first inside, desperate to find the toilets, closely followed by Connie and Chris. By the time we got back, we found the guys drinking pints and deciding what to order. I chose a seat diagonally to Eddie so I could see him well, but so I didn't have to actually eat in front of him, knowing he could see me square on. Whenever I looked at him, my legs went to jelly, and I did silly things like miss my mouth with my fork and shake when I pick up my glass. The thing is, he never noticed, and I doubted he ever would. I was clearly in the friend zone, and this meant I was so close to him I was sibling close, which for me was a huge bummer, to say the least.

We spent the next hour and a half eating and drinking with idle chit-chat. The food was real pub food with homemade chips and pastry for the pies. The veg was the obligatory peas with the thick-cut gammon and the eggs were plentiful, placed on top of the meat with runny yokes which exploded all over the juicy meat when cut into. The pies were full of thick; chunks of steak with tasty onions and rich gravy. We were so full after consuming the meals that we bought puddings to go along with peanuts and crisps for later.

We decided to drive on down to a town called Ville-De Place, right in the open countryside and a nice set of guest houses around it. It was about a three-hour drive and we took our stocks of food and drinks and placed them in the coolest part of the jeep between the luggage. Damon and Liam chose to share the driving on the first day, Eddie and Connie on the second, and Chris and me on the third.

It was about 6:30 p.m. when we finally saw the sign for Ville-De Place, and we stopped at a guest house invitingly named 'The Happy Lodger'. We booked our rooms and took our luggage up there. The landlady was called Martha and seemed very friendly. We asked if there was a pub nearby that served evening meals and she directed us to one, five doors down on the left.

After a brief wash and change, we met the guys in the foyer around 7:30 p.m. Martha waved us off and reminded us to be back before midnight as that was when she locked up. We eagerly strolled down the road, embracing the first day of our holiday. The streets were old and cobbled and there was a foreboding chill in the air.

Connie and Damon stopped so suddenly that the rest of us piled into them.

"What's going on?" demanded Liam who had stubbed his toe on the cobble stopping so suddenly.

"The pub," Damon said quietly.

"What about the goddam pub?" Retorted Liam.

"The name," said Connie. "Look."

We all looked up to meet the quite gruesome picture of a headless lamb, in the hands of a part-wolf part-monster type of creature. The name above this picture was, 'The Slaughtered Lamb'.

"Oops! Well, it looks a little scary but I'm sure it's fine, come on," said Chris, grabbing my hand, I, in turn, grabbed Eddie's.

Chapter Two
The Invitation

As we walked into the pub, we felt a cold chill, which lasted only for a minute and disappeared as soon as it had come. The pub was small, quaint, and full of character. The main feature was an open fireplace in the lounge area, surrounded by brass. The wooden beams were all around with brass decanters, various clocks, and strange crosses, all nailed up at odd angles and creating odd patterns. As we closed the door behind us, we noticed the crosses were also nailed to the door as if trying to keep something out. There was a welcoming smell of cigar smoke and slightly stale sweat, commonly associated with a pub atmosphere.

We ordered drinks from a rather jolly but stern-faced large lady behind the bar. She was keeping the male customers in line, dealing with their cheeky comments and affectionately telling them off. She recommended the slaughter special, stating it was worth the money, so we ordered six. We paid our bill, got the drinks, and sat down. Our conversation was hushed, and giggles stifled as everything else seemed quiet. There were plenty of people in the pub, it was crowded but it seemed as if someone was working a volume button. As soon as we entered the pub, somebody touched that button. Strange as this may seem; at first it was eerie but not uncomfortable. After about ten minutes, we became accustomed to it and fitted in quite happily.

I started a conversation up with some of the yokels about the pub and the meals they served. We discussed different dishes and types of beer. Conversation then went onto the brass crosses in the pub and the mute thing happened again. Instead of taking the hint, I went onto say how surprised we were that we had not seen any children running around the town and that was odd, especially as it was school holidays.

The barmaid spoke up from her position by the beer taps, "All bairns are inside and accounted for by 6 p.m., especially now the nights appears to be drawing in closer. That's what we do around here. It's safer for everyone, especially the bairns."

We giggled quietly but remained passive looking from then on, avoiding eye contact with any of the locals as we just thought they were all suffering from dementia. The rest of the evening was general chit-chat, discussing the food and how good it was and then how much we had enjoyed the journey so far. Around 11 p.m., we were just deciding to leave when the landlord approached Liam. He gave him a map with directions and after a lot of browbeating between them, they finally shook hands and Liam led us out the pub.

"Well, don't hold us in suspense what have you got? What was all that about?" asked Eddie.

"An invitation," said Liam smugly.

We all gathered around him as he spoke to us.

"We have been invited to an old run-down castle. The deal is, we spend two nights there and we get six meals on the house at the Slaughtered Lamb!" Explained Liam, in a triumphant voice.

"The things you will do for a free meal!" Laughed Damon.

"He'll do anything as long as he doesn't have to pay or cook it!" said Connie.

"Hang on you two," I said. "Where is this castle and what makes this landlord think we'll find it hard to spend two nights there?"

"The voice of reason…" said Liam. "The castle is situated on the other side of Hades Hill and according to local superstition, the building is doomed. No one will live in it because the undead still roams the estate during the night." Liam wore a sardonic grin while he told the rest of the story.

"A whole family was wiped out about twenty years ago. They were all found littered around the castle with various body parts missing. These excess limbs were found in the kitchen, neatly placed on the table ready to dice. There was blood everywhere and the killers were never caught. No one has lived in the house since, but plenty of locals have seen lights on in the windows and heard screeching and screaming. The children are all kept in at night after six were murdered on different occasions and found in the vicinity of the castle."

Christine's face went pale when she asked how the children died and an even lighter shade of pale when Liam told her.

"They were all butchered. Bite marks were found all over the bodies and bits were missing. Whoever did this worked up an appetite." Liam grinned.

Connie slapped Liam and I did my best to reassure her that it was all silly stories, and the locals were having a laugh with us possibly pulling a prank.

"We're not seriously stopping there, are we?" asked Eddie.

"Yes we are," said Liam, and Damon shouted, "Whooooopeee!"

So, the decision was made and our fate was determined that night for us to spend some time in the scary castle.

The rest of the evening was spent at the guest house, drinking hot coffee in our room. Girls' rooms are always tidier, so we suggested the boys come to ours with hot drinks and we discussed the next plans. We decided to leave after breakfast, at about 11 a.m. We were to make our way to Hades Hill and into the valley, beyond and up to the castle, following the map given to us by the Landlord. All we had to do was hang on to our nerves and stay there until Thursday morning. Our friendly landlord would come and check on us on Wednesday and Thursday morning, at about 8 a.m.

A pot of coffee later and we decided to turn in and call it a night. As all of us three girls were getting into bed, our conversation went back to the gruesome deaths.

"Do you really think any of the stories are true, Charlie?" asked Chris nervously.

"The deaths probably are true, but I would imagine the rest is just superstitious nonsense, made up, so the locals can have a laugh at outsider's expense," I answered.

"You know small-time gossip," said Connie. "Get some sleep, we will need to be up early tomorrow. Night girlies."

As sleep drew near, we were all filled with our thoughts about the next few days and what it was going to be like. Eventually, sleep took us all.

Chapter Three
The Journey

9 a.m. and we all met over the breakfast table. Hot tea and coffee, breakfast cereal, toast, fresh bread, bacon, sausage, eggs, and tomatoes adorned our senses and kept us occupied. We felt like royalty with such a feast laid out for us. Our nerves mixed with our excitement increased our appetites. We were still sitting there by 10 a.m.

Surprisingly enough, it was Chris who suggested we should get a move on and find the castle. Maybe she wanted to impress Liam with her newfound bravery, or maybe she just needed to convince herself that she possessed more backbone than she thought.

11 a.m. and we were all standing outside by the jeep. Martha came out, clutching a basket covered with a tea towel. She handed the basket to Damon, for whom I think, she had a soft spot.

"Two flasks of coffee and a bottle of pop. Choice of sandwiches, carrot cake, scones, and some fruit."

"Martha this is lovely, thank you so much but you didn't have to, you know," said Damon, radiating his usual charm.

"You kids be very careful out there. We don't have many visitors anymore and hardly any as nice as you six. Come back safe; the first sign of trouble, run home!" Martha warned us all, shaking her finger. She stayed outside waving us off, I thought I saw a tear in her eye, and this alarmed me, almost like she would never see us all again.

I looked around at everyone else to see if they saw anything, but they were all too busy chatting about the food in the basket and how nice it was of her to put it up for us.

As we set off, I and Eddie rummaged through our survival kits. We each had a rucksack and a torch. We split the first aid kit and we each had a bottle of water. We decided to keep the food together just to transfer it into a plastic bag so it would be easier to carry.

As we left the town behind us, we felt strangely vulnerable. There was so much open space and not a building in sight. The sky was a beautiful clear blue and without a cloud anywhere. The grass glowed green, making it appear youthful and flourished. The flowers were in little pockets of colour, sometimes looking like a grass rainbow. The birds were busy singing and everything appeared serene and peaceful. Bees buzzed around us frantic as ever and this reminded me even more that we were on vacation.

We had the roof off of the jeep and the warm breeze flowed through our hair. The air was filled with sarcastic laughter and wit. Everyone seemed on a high; a glorious day with six friends on an adventure.

The view from the jeep was magnificent. Open spaces as far as the eye could see. Hilly regions, deep valleys, forests dense with wildlife. There was so much to look at and so much to take in. Ladybugs were rife, they seemed to produce as you looked at them. Butterflies were in abundance, all of them in different colours but all having that unique resemblance, as though cloned.

We stopped the jeep to take some photos, to desperately catch the unique beauty on film. We all tried to get as many pictures as we could of that very moment, catching each other off guard with our cameras.

As we continued our journey, the conversation went onto the castle again. I secretly hoped that there would be a vagrant living there, just to add some excitement to our stay. Connie seemed to take all the stories seriously and she ferreted about in her bag until she pulled out her Swiss army knife.

"For protection," she said. We all laughed with her.

As we started to proceed up a slight incline, Liam informed us that we had reached Hades Hill. He had to shift the jeep down a gear to get us up the hill and we all appeared to be more sombre from here on in. The air appeared a little colder than before, almost a full degree under what it was. Liam slowed the jeep down so he could check instructions. Soon, we were at the top of the hill and a signpost pointed the way to 'Valley End'.

"This is it," said Liam and he turned the jeep towards the path indicated.

"'Valley End', what a strange name. Does it mean the end of the valley and here is a new one, or is it the end of the valley, or does it mean you are coming to the end of your journey or life?" Damon asked us all.

Chris said, "Great way to make me feel confident in looking forward to this, Damon!"

"My eagerness is slightly dampened now too," said Damon.

"Be quiet!" said Chris.

We all stopped talking and looked at Chris.

"Stop the jeep please Liam," she said quietly.

Liam pulled the vehicle over to one side.

"I don't hear anything Chris, just your voice!" said Liam, sounding frustrated.

"Exactly!" said Chris. "You don't hear anything because there is nothing to hear! Listen!"

I got out of the jeep, closely followed by everyone else. She was right, there was no sound at all, nothing to hear. There were no insects, no buzzing of bees, no crickets in the grass, nothing. I looked purposely in the grass and as mad as this sounds, no sign of ants or spiders, beetles, nothing at all.

What was most peculiar was the lack of birds. Not a single one to be seen anywhere. As we looked more fervently we noticed the extreme lack of flowers and the grass looked half-dead and off green with the soil appearing old, dry, and worn. The temperature was suddenly another degree lower, and we could feel the cold seeping through our hair and into our clothes threatening to hit flesh and bone.

"So, this is why they call it the 'Valley End'," said Damon quietly.

"Well, it is a sudden change to what we have driven through and it appears that nothing grows in Valley End. I vote we get back into the jeep and find this castle," I said, looking at everyone trying to silently encourage them all.

"Yeah, I second that," said Eddie and Damon, and they got into the jeep.

"Come on. The quicker we get there, the sooner we can eat," smiled, Damon.

We all giggled, and it eased the tension. Some of us emptied our bladders, behind the nearest bush, and then we set off. The conversation appeared forced to begin with but after about ten minutes, when we had all warmed up, we were back to normal again and seriously discussing why and how the terrain could be very different on this side of the valley.

We came up with many theories such as the Bermuda triangle, a desecrated ground, witchcraft, and alien invasion. All of these suggestions created further conversation and many laughs. Thus, making the long journey even shorter. We began to think that maybe, this part of the valley was in some sort of zone, and this was why we were experiencing these feelings. Maybe it was some sort of trick that the locals were playing on us and that it was all perfectly natural but something we couldn't explain but they could. The continued absence of birds and insects was too peculiar to ignore. The grass on either side of the jeep was there but didn't appear to be lush or alive; unable to breed bulbs and flowers almost what Astroturf would be like. Our thoughts took over the jeep again and we came back to the idea that everything isn't meant to live around this area and that would explain the absence of wildlife.

We seemed to be travelling for miles when we eventually saw the castle. It loomed up from nowhere and was large and menacing, with grey and brown turrets and dark windows. It looked quite threatening as it appeared to block out all the sky behind it and you could only seem to focus on the building.

We slowly crossed a dirt track and managed to pull the jeep up by the moat surrounding the castle.

Chapter Four

The Castle

As we stopped by the moat, the drawbridge started to lower, practically inviting us to board and cross into the confines of the castle itself. The bridge was huge and thick with old wood panels but sturdy enough to take a few vehicles across. There was no sign of anyone as we drove slowly across, and we wondered if it was worked by a possible pressure plate or whether the landlord was actually the other side but we hadn't seen him as yet. As our tires rolled over the wooden slats. We could hear them creaking but not in protest, it appeared to be in excitement. As one creaked the next also did, providing us with a strange drum roll, almost encouraging us to cross. As we crossed, the castle seemed to grow bigger in front of us. The original coldness of being in the valley appeared to dissipate and we felt a warm glow. The tops of the turrets seemed to grow taller, pushing themselves into the deep clouds and beyond.

We counted four big turrets, eight windows on the top one side, eight across the middle with six at the bottom. That's what we could see at the moment. The courtyard was huge and square with little benches around the edges but enough space to park several vehicles. I could imagine many parties being held here and coaches and horses being in tow. We got out of the jeep and looked around. Again, no flowers but tubs stood ready for them in special places all with soil in but nothing taking place in there.

"Well, are we going to just stand here?" said Connie. "Come on, let's explore." As if to support her, the still, warm air suddenly grew very cold, and a wind came from nowhere, making us shiver. We grabbed our belongings and the lunch that Martha had prepared for us and made our way up to the door.

And that was when we heard it, a loud screeching noise and a sound of flapping wings right close to us. As we looked up, we saw an incredibly large black raven flying low above our heads. It circled a few times, almost checking us out before coming to rest on the castle turret. Its beak was long and pronounced, and his eyes looked large and scary.

We frantically made our way to the door just as the wind blew a little harder. The door was huge with intricate carvings on the sides. The door knocker was shabby brass in the shape of a horseshoe with a brass wolf's head at the bottom of it. The head was just situated above eye level and appeared to look at you, wherever you stood. It had a peaceful face as if it belonged there, not a snarling aggressive face, so often associated with wolves.

I know from my studies that wolves will only attack if their territory is under threat or their young are in danger. They are carnivores but rarely tackle an animal bigger than themself and they never attack humans. The wolf instinct tells them to fear humankind because of man's intense hunger to hunt, maim and kill. I had always wanted to meet a wolf in real life and feel its close warm body next to mine, to befriend, to be trusted into the pack, to be at one with the wolf. What with all the myths and legends, and the hunters nowadays, my chances were running slim.

Sometimes man pisses me off, but I guess like someone once said to me – if you believe in God, he gave us the gift of life but he also gave us choice and man is greedy. So, God's a huge joker (my own opinion) he gave us a gift then sat back to watch us balls it all up!

Liam banged the knocker sending chills up our spines. The sound was low and guttural like it was entering the bowels of the earth.

"Nobody in," said Liam.

"Just open the damn door, Liam. I'm freezing my butt off here," wined Connie.

"Yes!" We all shouted together.

Liam turned the horseshoe to the right and gently pushed and with a slight resistance, the door opened.

As we entered the huge hallway, I looked closer at the door and under the wolf, it said, 'House of Lycan'. The rest of the wording was indistinguishable as the door was too dirty. I took out my hanky to try and rub off the excess dirt and Connie pulled me into the hall slamming the door.

"No time for cleaning, girl! We got a castle to investigate."

"Okay." I laughed. I loved her energy and her manic sense of adventure, and I threw down my bags and ran after her.

We ran from room to room with a childish surge for adventure and mischief and an innovative desire to explore. The castle was huge and vastly furnished. All of the furniture was covered with grey linen cloths which might have been white to start with. Settees, chairs, dining room tables, cabinets, beds, wardrobes, everything was covered. The beds were all made just covered for an eternity. The décor was exquisite in every room, including the bathrooms. Each room had a dado rail, matching wallpaper, and borders. It all blended in beautifully with the carpet and curtains. Every room had a plush carpet except the entrance hall and the ballroom. There were solid oak floors and were ceremoniously polished at one time. They were polished today which was odd. I was assuming, the landlord had given the place a clean-up before we arrived.

We found a beautifully furnished kitchen with a wood stove to cook upon. Pots and pans were hanging up and a large copper kettle made us think of hot tea and carrot cake. There was a floating cupboard in the centre of the room, and this was accompanied by high stools to serve as a breakfast bar as well as the huge circular kitchen table and set of eight chairs.

As we explored further, opening cupboards and drawers, we found cups, plates, dishes, and cutlery. There was a large pantry stocked with tins, rice, and some fresh vegetables. There was also a cooked gammon joint wrapped in cling film and ready to eat with a note on it saying, "Our guests, please enjoy."

I found this odd as it was left in the pantry, not on the side so we would see it, but I was thankful for the kindness of the landlord, leaving it there for us. He knew we loved our food.

The men decided to go out and get some kindling and logs from the wood bunker in the courtyard while we girls sorted lunch that Martha had set up for us. We also got the gammon out and sliced generous pieces for everyone, wrapping the rest up to keep fresh. With fresh coffee and tea and slices of carrot cake for afters, we felt blessed.

All of a sudden, there was a knock from the front door which seemed to rock the whole building. Connie opened the door to the landlord of the Slaughtered Lamb.

"Hello," he said as he took his hat off. "I'm Jake and this is my son, Mitchell."

We all greeted Jake and Mitchell, who was shockingly similar to his father. He was stocky with black curly hair, large eyes, and a mischievous grin.

"I brought you all some tea and coffee and a few tins and things to tide you over, that's if you stay that long," Jake said with a glint in his eye.

"Oh, we'll be staying, we like it here already." Grinned Connie.

"Help yourselves to sandwiches and cake, guys." Offered Chris.

"That's great! Thank you, don't mind if we do," said Jake.

"Oh and thank you for cooking the joint of gammon for us. That was a lovely thought. Help yourself to some." I offered.

Both Jake and Mitchell looked a little confused then wary but only for a brief second before saying, "It's not a problem."

"What did you mean when you said, 'if we stay'?" I asked Jake.

"Well young bairn, it's about time I told you the whole story, all of you." Jake's tone turned serious.

"Remember I said about twenty years ago, the whole family was wiped out?" he said. We all nodded in unison.

"Well, there have been several deaths, all mysterious and grizzly since then. All of the killings have happened in and around this castle."

We all listened, and our mood grew more serious. Jake went on to tell us the story of events. When the Need family came to their unfortunate end, the whole town of Hades went numb with shock. The one undertaker in the town was the only person with a smile on his face. He never had so much business pushed his way, in fact, over the next few years not only did business improve, but more staff had to be taken on to cope with the workload.

Every town had a haunted house and Hades was no exception. The castle was the typical haunted house. Children and young teenagers played games of terror hide and seek around the grounds of the building and the surrounding woodlands. Eventually, with the obvious murders unsolved and the castle still locked and boarded up, curiosity got the better of the young mischievous locals. The yellow police tape was torn away from the doors and a lower floor window smashed to allow entry if you were successful in getting across the moat and through the bridge.

Kids dared each other to spend a night there and in playing their childish games; rooms, furniture, and windows were trashed. This was about six months after five young lads decided to stay the night in the castle. At the time, the town was called 'Petit Heaven', as it addressed and described the beauty of it all in just two simple words. The boys kept to their decision and stayed the night. Only one survived and he is in a mental institution in Caine. His name is Neil Davids, and he was found running through the streets of Petit Heaven at 5 a.m., babbling about monsters and completely naked. The local Sheriff was notified and at about 9:30 a.m. accompanied by his deputy, he entered the castle through the lowered draw bridge.

Everything was quiet and nothing seemed to match the boy's story. He described the inside of the castle as run down and messy with blood everywhere smeared across walls and the floors. Bodies were meant to be strewn everywhere of lots of dead people from time ago. Downstairs appeared to be okay and they made their way upstairs to the first floor.

Deputy Winston found the one boy sitting on the toilet with his throat cut and the entrails, slipping freshly down the side of the bowl, disembowelled. Sheriff Charles found the other three boys in one of the bedrooms on the same floor. All three had their throats cut and they were propped up in sitting positions with their hands almost touching, in a parody of affection. All three were naked. There was visible bruising on all the bodies but not a lot of blood as one would expect with such a gruesome murder.

The rest of the castle was checked out and nothing seemed out of place. Parts of the building even seemed to have been restored. If there was blood anywhere else, like the Davids' kid said, it was certainly not there when the cavalry arrived.

The bodies were taken over to Maine for a full examination, while the grounds were checked out with a fine-tooth comb. The only evidence of anything other than the four lads being in the castle were a few coarse long black and grey hairs, later to be found to have belonged to an animal of some kind. Semen stains were found by the door, later identified as originating from a wild animal, possibly lupus/canine variety. The boys loved their dogs so it was seen as possible that dogs may have been inhabiting the grounds at some point and were unrelated to this case.

The coroner's report was just as strange. All four boys had died due to having their throats cut and suffering a great loss of blood from the jugular vein. The incisions were very neat. Boy number one, the boy on the toilet, was disembowelled just before his jugular was severed. The clavicle bruising showed how he was restrained while his insides slipped in and around the toilet bowl. Just when his pain and suffering had probably reached a height of no return, he would have been relieved into a blissful bloodless sleep and wouldn't have felt his throat being expertly sliced.

Boy number two, found propped up against the bed, was practically beaten to death. There was extensive bruising to the lower body probably produced by savage kicking. He sustained a ruptured liver and spleen. A ballpoint pen was found broken off in his anal cavity, causing deep tearing of the bowel. Most of the facial bones were broken and only then did the perpetrator feel compassion to blissfully slice the jugular and end the suffering.

Boy number three suffered in silence, his tongue was cleanly taken out and replaced by his penis, also neatly dissected. Bite marks were found all over the upper part of the torso. The bruising caused by the bite marks had spread into the tissues, so disguising, the biter's teeth. Unfortunately, no impressions could be made. Again, the throat was cut.

Boy number four showed clear signs of asphyxia. Body temperature had risen, the skin was dusky on his head and neck, and pinhead haemorrhages were very clear in the scalp, indicating an obstruction of breathing for at least 20 seconds. Finally, the throat had suffered the same fate as the other boys. The killer had obviously reached boredom by the fourth victim as bloodless wounds were found all over the lower trunk, indicating post-life activity. Animal excrement was found packed in the nose and mouth, the cause of the asphyxia.

A full investigation took place, but nothing came of it. Locals wanted the castle torn down, but it had a preservation order on it. It was boarded up again and signs were erected all around it, warning people to 'Keep Out'.

A few months later, a Kurt Barlow from Germany, took over the castle and the arduous task of renovation and upkeep. No one knew much about him except his nationality and the fact that he was a billionaire. He liked his privacy and rarely entered the town. He was supposed to work in antiques and only came to the castle every two months or so. He would stay with his butler Jameson for a few days and then they would return to the hustle and bustle of selling.

Jameson was very quiet and a loyal servant. He would visit the town to collect local delicacies and was often seen walking Barlow's beloved dog, Lightning, a long-haired husky. A couple of years passed uneventfully and then all of a sudden, children started to go missing. They were all said to have been playing near the castle. No trace was ever found of these children and no one could be held responsible. Barlow and Jameson were out of town when each disappearance took place. Barlow allowed police to search the grounds and the building thoroughly so he could aid the search party, but nothing was ever found.

Soon superstition surrounded the castle and locals would say the reason Barlow only visited occasionally and for such a short while was that he was afraid to stay longer. Eventually, the locals decided to change the town name, which they did to Hades as it was the exact opposite to Heaven. The disappearances were put down to possible slave trade, rumoured to be in operation on the coast. This was pure speculation and nothing else.

The antique business soared and Barlow found himself away on business more. He entrusted Jake and his family to keep an eye on the place and he left them the keys with an ample yearly payment for their services. He also permitted Jake, to let people stay short term as he preferred the castle to be lived in.

"When was Mr Barlow last here?" asked Eddie.

"Two weeks ago," answered Jake. "He usually comes here about once a month. He doesn't mind people staying here as long as you respect the place and I know you will."

"What makes you think we'll chicken out and not stay?" asked Connie.

Jake shrugged his shoulders and looked at his son and said "We wager you six meals on the house that you don't stay. It's just a bit of fun."

"Jake, what is the castle called?" I asked.

"House of Lycanthrope," answered Jake. "Mr Barlow loves his wolves. He has one as a pet and he adorns his walls with still photographs of them. He likes the way they stick together as a family and are loyal to the core and protective of what they own."

"Fascinating," said Liam, "although, I haven't seen any pictures."

"No," I said, "Neither have I."

Jake shrugged his shoulders again, "Oh well we must be going. See you all in the morning at about 8:30 a.m. Oh, and er… sleep tight, pleasant dreams."

"Bye." We all chorused.

"Well," said Eddie, "let's look at what we can put together for tea."

We didn't realise but we had been sitting chatting for over two hours with Jake and his son and time had flown by. The name change of the town was the big topic strangely enough, not the actual deaths. Things must have been bad for the locals to change the actual name of where they live because of tragic events.

It went from Petit Heaven which I thought was possibly meaning of a small taste of heaven to Hades. He was known as the god of the Underworld, son of the Titans, Cronus, and Rhea. He had three sisters; Demeter, Hestia, and Hera, as well as two brothers, Zeus; the youngest of the three, and Poseidon. Following the overthrow of first, the Titans and then the Giants by the Olympian gods, Hades drew lots with his brothers, Zeus and Poseidon, to decide which part of the world each would rule. Zeus received the sky, Poseidon the seas, and Hades the Underworld. It is said that Hades had no choice but to take control of the Underworld as his brothers had chosen the other two. Hades has been thought to mean the 'Unseen One'. He ruled the Underworld and had control over the dead and riches (metals and precious stones), and as such had some power over the earth.

I felt maybe the town was called Hades as whatever was happening, was being done by someone unseen and it was clearly an evil act and linked with the absence of flowers and life in the grass and meadows, etc. It was felt to be dead ground. I voiced my opinions with everyone else and they too agreed, it could have been like this.

Chapter Five

Settling In

After a hearty meal of warmed-up meatloaf, beans, and crusty bread, we decided to retire to the library. Liam had a roaring log fire going and the whole room looked very inviting. There were candles everywhere, reminding us the castle did not have electricity. In the cold light of day, the building was magnificent, spacious, and homely but as night drew in around us and the candles were lit, it suddenly became foreboding. All of those dark corners suddenly became menacing shadows and our thoughts returned to the bloodshed that had occurred.

We avoided the room that the boys were supposed to have died in and settled for six of the others. The bathroom, unfortunately, we could not avoid, and the others were further away so we used it. Still, we all double-checked it before we were comfortable. We all retired to our rooms with candles, matches, and hot drinks.

Each room was large and spacious, and they were all situated on the same floor. The room we avoided was at the bottom of the hall, next to the bathroom. The stairs were at the end of the corner, next to the toilet. As we disappeared into our rooms, we waved to each other and closed our doors.

I climbed into bed, feeling the cleanness of the sheets and loving how crisp white everything was. I settled down and closed my eyes. I awoke throughout the night hearing general noises of the castle as it prepared to sleep; creaking of floorboards, the sound of the wind whistling past the windows, and the pitter-patter of rain, accompanied with the odd banging of a shutter somewhere in the building.

As I lay there I became accustomed to these noises, and I accepted them as the norm. Becoming familiar with the nightly sounds was easier than I thought it would be. What did bother me was the unfamiliar surroundings; the different shapes of furniture casting shadows across the room, the thin curtains eerily reflecting the moon. The warm glow from the fore was casting a yellowy gleam around the room, making the brass knockers on the chest of drawers stand out.

The bed was large and very comfortable, and pillows were generously packed with soft feathers. The bedding was a brilliant starched white colour and smelt ever so slightly musky but pleasant. As my curiosity of the new surroundings came to a close, sleep became imminent and my eyelids lost the battle with gravity.

Chapter Six
Night One

Scratching, that annoying sound that seems to disassociate itself with your eardrums and become a constant stab of displeasure. As I slowly came to, my eyes still hoping to remain in sleep-land, the scratching became louder and more insistent. It sounded like a myriapod with numerous leg-bearing segments (but I know centipedes don't have the equipment needed to scratch).

The sound wasn't coming from one particular place but all corners of the room. This was not only frightening in itself but the realisation that I could be surrounded woke me up! I groped around on the dressing table and came into contact with a spare candle and matches. After two failed attempts I eventually managed to strike a match and the room came into focus. I lit the candle and examined the room visually. Nothing seemed out of place. I started to walk slowly around the room, listening intently, my eyes beginning to burn with the poor light. After a thorough check, I found no gaps in the floorboards, walls, and skirting boards. No secret passages and nothing under the bed, chest of drawers, or other oddments of furniture.

Without any visible signs of evidence relating to a rodent or such, but still, with constant scratching available to any working eardrum, I felt less than reassured. I wanted so much to find a simple answer and instead, I just found myself asking more questions. I stamped my foot in despair and decided to go back to bed and blot out the sound. I pulled the covers up and around my chin and snuggled up to myself, hoping that by keeping warm and comfortable, I would eventually be taken over by sleep and therefore, forget the annoying sound. About twenty minutes later, however, I became fully alert.

The noise had stopped! I lay there for what seemed like an eternity hearing nothing. I then found myself thinking I had imagined the whole thing in the first place. As I was filled with a strange sense of relief, I also became aware of my need for fluid. My throat felt like sandpaper and I knew I wouldn't be able to wait until the morning. I decided to get a glass of water from the kitchen. I put on my housecoat and armed with my candles and box of matches, made my way onto the landing. As I approached the stairs, I carefully checked in all directions, not quite knowing what I was looking for but being cautious all the same.

Just then a door opened, and a shaft of light appeared on the landing. Liam stood there, looking sleepy but wary. "Oh, it's you. I knew I heard something. What are you doing?"

"I want a glass of water. I'm sorry if I woke you," I whispered, careful not to wake anyone else.

"That's okay, I'll come with you," Liam said.

He came out with his housecoat, half on pulling it right and grunting with tiredness. We made our way down the stairs, keen not to wake anyone. Liam was close at my heels, and I could feel his hot breath on my neck, making me feel strangely violated. Here I was with a persistent company, in the early hours of the morning when all I really wanted was to be alone with my thoughts.

I opened the kitchen door and Liam said, "Hang on, I can't walk that fast in the dark."

"Liam, you were right at my heels on the stairs."

"I wasn't, I was struggling to see the stairs," Liam said as I waited for him to go into the kitchen first.

He picked up two glasses out of the cupboard and I said I could tell he was right behind me on the stairs as I could feel him breathing over my neck. He looked past me, towards the door not saying anything. I followed his gaze moving my candle to allow more light to shine in that direction. I saw two green eyes staring back at me. A low guttural growl came out of the figure. Liam screamed and dropped the glasses. I turned to see if he was alright and when I shone the candle back towards the door, our visitor had gone. I thought I heard padded footsteps but couldn't be sure. I helped Liam pick up the glass and we sat at the table. He was physically shaking from head to toe. I got more candles out of the kitchen drawer and lit them, standing them up in saucers. Liam just sat there, looking at the kitchen door fearfully. We both nearly jumped out of our skin as the stairs creaked and shadowy figures stood in the entrance to the kitchen.

"What the hell is happening?" Connie said. "Don't you invite your friends to your parties?"

Suddenly everyone burst into the room, laughing and joking around. Everyone, except for me and Liam. When this became apparent to everyone, they quickly sat around the table and waited for us to speak.

Liam did not take his eyes off of the door as he told everyone about the growl and the shadowy shape he saw. Questions were asked and conversation for the next half hour was solemn. I didn't find it necessary to tell everyone about the eyes of the animal that I felt were only looking at me. I found it odd that Liam hadn't seen them, and I was beginning to doubt myself.

Edward lit the stove and put a kettle of water on it as Chris organised cups and tea bags. It was 3:15 a.m. and the six of us were awake and partaking in tea and biscuits. Liam finally calmed down and occasionally looked at the door as if he thought it may come back. Damon and Eddie walked out into the hall and checked the door and the windows and found them all secure. If there was something out in the hall, then it had been with us since we arrived. We decided to split into twos and check all the rooms.

I was surprised how well Christine was taking all this, normally she came across as timid and easily frightened but as I watched her walk off with Liam to start checking rooms. She had a purpose and a strength to her stride and a reassuring calmness to her voice as she chatted with Liam, who had become a lot less furtive.

Damon and I checked upstairs, while Connie and Eddie checked and scouted around downstairs. We all met up on the stairs, obvious relief showing on everyone's faces.

"Well, nothing seems to be amiss," said Connie. "So, I now suggest that we all check the upper floor together."

Nodding in agreement, we gathered our candles and made our way to the end of the hall, where we found another flight of stairs. With Connie in the lead, we all climbed the stairs and found ourselves on another landing, much the same as the one below. There was a cold chill in the air and the noise of the wind was much louder on this floor. Very quickly and efficiently, we opened every door and had a peek in each room. As we closed the last door, we again gave a sigh of relief.

"Come on let's go and get a cup of coffee," said Eddie. "We'll find all this very funny in the morning."

"It is morning!" I exclaimed after looking at my watch. It was 5:45 a.m., we had been searching for over two hours!

"Well, not much point going to bed," laughed Connie.

"Bed? What's bed?" laughed Damon.

In a giggly state, we all went back downstairs, and very soon, hot tea was served with toast and cereal. We didn't talk much about the hours that just passed and I got the feeling that everyone thought it had been a figment of our imagination. Chat was light and cheerful, and plans were made to explore the castle further and the grounds.

As everyone dispersed to get washed and dressed, Liam came over to me. "What I saw was real, you know," he looked me straight in the face and sounded sombre and earnest.

"I know it was, remember I was there with you, but we both were tired too." I turned to put my dish in the sink.

Liam grabbed my arm a little too hard and grimaced between clenched teeth, "I know what I saw, I know what I saw. There's something in this castle and that's a fact!"

I just stared at him, unable to utter a single word. I had never seen anyone so shaken. I watched him turn and walk upstairs, looking around him furtively. I was exhausted; my head was starting to make its own tune, like an incessant drum roll. Exactly what had I seen last night, everything seemed a little vague in the light of day. Suddenly I noticed the silence, the rain had completely stopped, and the wind was mild. I decided to go out for a walk and clear my head. After dressing quickly, I was out before anyone knew I had gone. Solitude was what I needed, what I craved at that moment, to clear my head and get some perspective.

The wind was soft against my jacket and even though chilly, it freshened me up nicely, making me feel vitalised. I started to walk around the castle grounds, towards the moat on the far side. This was a dense forest and had not been tended to in a while. I kept walking straight so I wouldn't get lost and very soon, I came to a small clearing where two tyres were hanging from thick, sturdy trees swinging gently in the breeze. This was a child's hideaway, to play without being spotted by the castle inhabitants. The tyres were old and the rope haggard, but it seemed strong enough to do the job. I soon had myself wrapped around one of them, swinging in the breeze.

My thoughts went to the previous night, and I started to remember how it began. I had trouble sleeping due to scratching noises in the room, but I couldn't see anything, and then I was thirsty, so I went down to the kitchen to get a drink. I had met Liam on the landing, and I wondered now, why he was awake and if he had heard the same noises as me.

I heard a twig snap, and I swung the tyre around sharply, falling off in my haste to see what was behind me. I landed on my rump with a thud on the hard ground and I yelped sharply. Looking around, towards the sound, I saw two eyes staring back at me. These belonged to an extremely large wolf. Grey and silver coloured and sharply chiselled features. It walked towards me quiet and majestic, never taking his eyes from my face. Stopping about five yards away, sniffing the air cautiously he kept his eyes on me. I stared back, staying as still as possible and almost holding my breath. The sound of my heart beating hard in my chest seemed to be drumming in my ears. The animal came so close to me that our noses were almost touching and my heart almost stopped when the large snout opened, and a pink tongue delicately travelled from my chin up to my forehead. I closed my eyes, feeling the roughness of the tongue and the hot breath on my face.

When I opened my eyes, I was alone. I looked around, alarmed, trying to find my new friend and I saw the back of his huge frame walking away from me, back through the forest away from the castle. I followed him, anxious to not lose him and to feel that animal closeness that left me feeling loved, excited, and whole. I felt I had come so close to danger, twice now and the thrill was alluring. I ran after him as fast as I could, always keeping him in sight but never quite managing to catch up. I seemed to go for miles, and I knew this was not possible, surely the edge of the moat would appear any time now but I was going deeper and deeper into the forest. Eventually, I stumbled into a clearing and stopped suddenly as he was right in front of me.

He was sat on his haunches, looking relaxed just staring at me. I steadied myself on a tree nearby and wiped my sleeve across my forehead, collecting beads of perspiration. I looked at where I found myself and was aghast at the sight. I was in a small but neat cemetery. There were about seven visible gravestones and upon careful searching, I could see a few more. The initial seven were in a circle and the grass had been tended to keep them looking neat and preserved with each stone clean and polished. The clearing itself was very prominent, with the grass on the outside of the circle being a deeper green in colour and a lot longer, some as high as the gravestones scattered in it.

By this time, my furry friend had settled down on the grass, so I took this opportunity to walk around the stones carefully reading any epitaphs. They were all very old and some clearer than others. One read:

"Presbyter Arnold Wolfgang

Founder of our Episcopal Church.

May God be with you."

No dates were telling me when they had died, and this was the same for all the graves.

"Freud stein William.

Master of Lycanthrope Castle.

Home to Wolf and Master.

May you be a part of this castle for always."

Lycanthrope, of course, was what was inscribed on the castle door, meaning werewolf. A person who suffers from lycanthropy is supposed to actually feel the sensation of changing from one form into another, from man to wolf. There was a connection here, between the castle, the graves, and the wolf. Maybe, my little friend had just lost his master or maybe this is where he lived, by the graves of his ancestors.

Suddenly, shrill voices broke the silence of the place, and I heard my name being called over and over. I felt a slight tug on the finger of my left hand and the wolf was trying to pull me away. All at once, he scampered off into the undergrowth, and Liam, Eddie, and Connie closely followed by Chris and Damon bust through the trees.

"Where the bloody hell have you been?"

"How dare you just walk off?"

"What do you think you're playing at?"

"We care about you! Don't you know that?" Liam threw his arms around me and had tears in his eyes.

I was overwhelmed with emotion and the feelings my friends had for me. I didn't know what to say. Connie said, "We've been shouting and shouting your name and then we find you in a graveyard!"

"I know, I'm really sorry, guys, to just walk off. I needed some air and then I came upon this. It appears to be the dead relatives and owners of the castle."

"Inside the circle maybe but not over here," said Eddie and we all walked to where he was.

"My God! They're all victims of the castle murders," said Chris in a shocked voice.

"I guess when they died, the villagers decided to have their remains put here, the last place they were alive," Damon said solemnly.

"Weird!" said Connie. "Oh, God! Listen to this! Here lies the body of Rachel Dennington. Died at the brutal hands of another. Her soul will forever lay in these castle grounds and her memory will linger on as an eternal cloud."

"Wow, deep stuff. I think we should get back, it's getting cold," suggested Chris.

We all started walking; arms linked, trying to keep warm due to the sudden temperature drop. It was quite a long trek back. I didn't realise how far I had come, being alone with my thoughts, distance didn't appear to be an obstacle. By the time we had reached the castle, we were exhausted and cold. Hot chocolate and the carrot cake were consumed heartily. Our conversation was about last night's antics and why I had disappeared on my own this morning.

I decided to tell everyone about the scratching noises in my room and was quite amazed to hear that they had also heard strange sounds. Connie had heard strange shifting noises like furniture being moved from one place to another. It lasted about 30 minutes and she just assumed that it was either one of us or it was related to the horrendous wind rocking the shutters. Damon and Chis slept fitfully until 3 a.m. when they heard talking and came downstairs to find us in the kitchen. Eddie had heard soft thudding but it didn't keep him awake but Damon woke him up to tell him to come downstairs. It made me feel better knowing that others had had their sleep disturbed too. We decided the castle must be haunted as there was no physical evidence of a flesh and blood intruder.

As we had been up half the night, we decided to take a nap. Everyone went off to their rooms and I decided to rest on the couch in the lounge. The room was dark green in décor and had a comfortable feel to it. I lay there for ten minutes before I felt my eyes begin to close and I gave in to the urge to sleep gracefully.

Chapter Seven
The Cellar

A good hour had passed before I woke, my neck stiff, having lain at an awkward angle. Throwing my legs off the settee, I sat up and decided a hot cup of coffee would appease me. Standing in the kitchen, waiting for the water to heat up, I happened to look at the window. Five figures were standing across the moat staring at the castle. They didn't move a muscle, just stood there gawping.

Just then, a loud noise came from the cellar in the corner of the kitchen. I decided to find out what was down there. I had to struggle with the door as it was so stiff and heavy. Grabbing the torch from the side, I made my way down the cold concrete steps into more blackness below. I had enough light to make out a wine rack, a workbench, and numerous pieces of wooden furniture. My beam found its way to some brass objects like door knockers, pokers, kettles, etc. My curiosity was aroused and I went for a closer look.

Suddenly, a few soft bumps followed by a sickening crack made me look towards the stairs. In the light from my torch, I saw a sight that I would never forget. Liam's decapitated head lay by my feet, its sinews and bloody entrails threatening to crawl over my shoes. His eyes still held a horrifying glazed look and his tongue laid out of his mouth, blood starting to congeal around his lips.

I stuffed my fist into my mouth to stifle any screams that might escape and I ran to hide behind the wine rack. Fighting to keep the vomit down, as I tasted the first wave as it made its way up my gullet, I fought to breathe making more noise trying to regulate and I switched off the torch. I stayed there, crouched behind dusty wine bottles, quivering with fright. It was pure fear that prevented the sickness and kept me in the same spot. I was numb with exhaustion and fright and lost all sense of time.

I came to when the cellar door banged shut. Realising I was now quite alone, I peed myself and vomited in quick succession. I retched until I thought it would become possible to sick up my internal organs. Sitting back on my haunches I reached for my torch and wiped my mouth on my cardigan sleeve. I knew I had to keep calm, if not for my sake, but for everyone else still in the castle.

Slowly I tiptoed over to Liam, switched on the torch, gripping it tightly, afraid that I might drop it and involuntarily scream. In the newfound light, I saw my friend all too clearly. My poor, poor Liam. The only difference this time to when I saw him last was the torso lying askew at the bottom of the stairs. It looked like some sort of cosmic horror where the jigsaw pieces were human. God, I was losing my mind.

The cut looked clean and I just hoped he hadn't suffered. I closed his eyes and muttered a quick prayer. I felt myself sobbing softly and knew I wouldn't be able to stop so I sat next to my friend until my tears slowed and my body ceased to quiver. I knew I had to get out of the cellar before whatever it was that had killed Liam returned. But there was a problem, whoever murdered Liam was somewhere in the castle. Maybe I was safer staying where I was. The smell of death was already quite strong, and I didn't relish the idea of inhaling Liam until help arrived; if it was going to arrive. A big 'if' with a capital I. Jake was due to come tomorrow morning. I didn't think I could last that long. My mind shot back to the people staring at the castle. They didn't look especially friendly, maybe they had something to do with all this.

Listening intently, I climbed the stairs being aware of every crack and soft footfall and feeling my heart pounding in my chest. I stood behind the door listening, hearing no noise I turned the knob, counted to three then threw my weight against the solid wood. The door opened creaking loudly. I immediately closed it and ran for the kitchen drawer, taking out a large bread knife. Clutching my weapon for dear life, I entered the hall and frantically looked around. Nothing. No-one. No sign of life at all.

Cautiously I checked out the ground floor and on finding nothing decided to look upstairs. As I climbed up I became aware of being very much alone. I opened every room and found no one. My friends had either left me or had been taken somewhere. I went back to my room and closed the door. Looking out the window, I noticed the people had gone. I could leave now, go out the door across to the jeep, grab the spare set of keys (which were always under the passenger seat) and get drive like hot shit off a shovel and never look back. I could, but I knew I wouldn't, not without my friends. Where the hell were they?

I decided to lie low in my room just for a while. Maybe if I was patient and stayed calm, things would work out. I noticed my glass of squash was still next to my bed and I sipped greedily. Being sick always made me feel thirsty. I sat on the bed still clutching the knife and waited.

And waited and waited. Suddenly feeling very tired, exhausted, I dropped off to sleep.

Chapter Eight
Hunger

I felt a hot breath kiss my lips and my nose. My eyelids wanted to open but were helplessly shut. Wispy tendrils of hair stroked my neck sending chills up my spine. I felt soft lips kiss my toes and ankles, a slippery tongue traced its way up my calves and behind my knees. My legs were pulled apart gently but meaningfully and I longed for my moistness to be penetrated. As if sensing my feelings, my sexual organs were avoided. I found myself frustrated and angry and decided that I didn't like dreams much anymore. Then I suddenly had a warm slippery sensation over my already erect nipples and could feel teeth nibbling delicately. I pushed my dream to the limits, imagining Eddie's face pressed to mine, his tongue probing the recess of my mouth, and his hot sex pressing against my tummy.

Urgently I took over and I knew an orgasm was imminent. I opened my legs wider and felt his penis penetrate my warm crevice. I bucked to accept him and he thrust harder. Eventually, I orgasmed screaming Eddie's name over and over again. I felt him release and I lay there in the final pleasurable moment of my dream.

A cold chill swept over me and I opened my eyes. I felt slow and dizzy. Sitting up, I gradually came to and wished I'd stayed asleep.

My whole chest was covered in small black hairs, my inner thighs had what looked like a mixture of blood and semen and next to my right leg lay a severed penis. The purple end normally bulbous and erect was limp and seeping blood. The trunk end was covered in blood and bits of torn flesh lay around it. I screamed and screamed for what seemed like an eternity, grabbing the already bloody sheet and wrapping it around myself as I leaped up from the bed. Feeling a wave of dizziness come over me, I grabbed the bedpost for support and threw the sheet over the bed hiding the mess to block it out momentarily.

Coming slowly to, I took in my surroundings. I didn't recognise the room. The furniture was still covered in white sheets and the bed was a four-poster. It suddenly dawned on me that this was the bedroom we had avoided, the one where the boys had died. Already feeling violated, my nakedness meant nothing. I began to look around the room, carefully avoiding the bed. The room was completely empty and that scared me. From the hungover feeling, I couldn't shake. I came to the conclusion I had been drugged. Then stripped of my clothes (of which there was no sign) and taken to a different room. I had then had sex with a dismembered penis which in itself was incredible. Either the person making love to me got turned on by using another man's tool or he was dickless and bleeding to death. I heard myself chuckle and realised I was closer to cracking up than I thought. Someone was playing with me. They/he/she could probably see me now. Had probably been watching me since I got here, but strangely enough, they didn't want to kill me, not yet anyway. I walked out of the room and up the corridor into my room that had been for the past one night. I was surprised to see all my clothes had gone apart from one pair of blue faded jeans and a pink woollen jumper. I also spotted my dirty trainers. I grabbed all my stuff and ran to the bathroom. Five minutes later I emerged cleaner and dressed.

I made my way downstairs and grabbed my coat off the hat stand and left the castle. I made my way to the clearing where I had seen the wolf. I knew the answer to all of this lay somewhere there.

Chapter Nine

Secrets

As I neared the spot where all of the graves were, the light had begun to fade and I noticed how quiet everything became. I started to feel eerie and the stone epitaphs became more prominent. The decadence of the place was particularly overwhelming and I felt as if all of the past souls were looking down on me, feeding on my fears and my loneliness. Newfound anger settled over me and lay heavy in my stomach as I realised I was being manipulated by someone I hadn't even met!

My friends, I had to assume were all dead, taken out of this world without their consent. I was left as a little pawn in a big man's world, scared shitless at seeing one and possibly two of my closest friends dead, sexually used, drugged without compliance, waking up to the knowledge of just being invaded by a recently detached penis! I started to giggle out loud, frightening myself even more. The sound of my hysterical laughter seemed so out of place next to such death, horror, and debris.

As I quietened myself, struggling to take hold of my detached emotions, I realised I was being watched. A man of average size and stature, wearing a long camel coloured coat with thick brown boots waved at me, signalling for me to follow him. I had nothing to lose, I was already lost so I made my way over to him. He had sharp pronounced features and long brown/blond hair to his shoulders looking a little Neanderthal. He was difficult to place an age on and he walked with great purpose and agility seemingly possessing the strength and energy of a man at least twenty years his junior. I had to run to keep up with him and I panicked in case I lost him. Sadly, this stranger was all I had left.

I followed him until we came to a brick building with a fire lit just outside. Sat around the warm glow were five other figures, seven as soon as my stranger and I sat down. I looked around at everyone, five men and one woman, all of them looking quite normal. Each one smiled at me in turn, seemingly friendly, supportive expressions on their countenance. I was completely perplexed, what did these people want from me?

Suddenly out of the building came a man about 6ft tall, quite bony in build with long grey/white hair tied in a band at the nape of his neck. He wore a long black coat and had on dark clothes underneath. He walked with a silvery cane and by his side stood a wolf. A beautiful grey and silver animal of amazing proportions. He was extremely large and held his head high in a majestic fashion. His legs looked strong and nimble and his paws large and splayed out to accommodate his great stature. Everyone raised their heads to greet the tall man as he walked closer, the light from the fire casting shadows over his face making him look waxen and smooth.

"I see we have a visitor," he spoke with a deep, hypnotic drawl. "Thank you for joining us. I see you recognise my friend." He tapped on the wolf's head delicately.

"I have a lot to tell you, Charlie. I'm not all bad and I hope you will understand that, in the end."

As he crouched opposite me, the wolf came and lay down by my feet. I stayed quiet, not quite knowing what to say and suddenly, feeling that I must wait for permission before uttering a sound. The man possessed great power but not all of it frightening. He also had a calming effect which seemed to almost hypnotise.

"We have been living here for over a hundred years and in that time, have seen many, many faces and many changes, some good, some bad."

As he began talking I got myself comfortable and absently stroked the wolf at my feet, who responded by placing his head in my lap.

"We were living in a part of the castle, working for the Freud stein family, an elderly couple with a child. They decided to have just the one as he was a bit of a social misfit. Not quite all there and he needed constant attention and various nurses were assigned to this unenviable task. We, as a family grew and grew, staying in the servant's quarters and tending to the needs of our employers. We served as the butler, maid, domestic, cook, and sometimes maid to the child if he was left in the lurch which was often the case.

The child's name was Eilrahc, pronounced Hierarch, as in hierarchy; an important person of noble blood. As a youngster, he seemed odd but his actions got worse the older he became. He started to get into insect torture then moved swiftly onto rabbits and larger animals that he could get his hands on. He seemed to want to be the power source to everything to make decisions over life and death.

When he was about sixteen, his desires turned sexual. He didn't get his kicks out of torturing defenceless creatures anymore. Those feelings he had grew more and more urgent until one day the inevitable happened. A young girl was found on the moors quite dead. She had been raped and tortured sexually in a horrific way and every orifice was filled with semen and faeces. Tests revealed both substances to be from Eilrahc. The girl was fourteen years of age and said to be promiscuous. This helped Eilrahc immensely especially when he was diagnosed as mentally retarded. He was sent away to a hospital for the mentally ill in Castle ridge about fifteen miles away. His sentence was to be for seven years, only to be reviewed and resentenced again.

The community was in total shock and everyone mourned the little girl and did their best to comfort the family. The Freud steins moved away for a while to let the dust settle and returned a few months later to a much happier scene with strange circumstances. The girl's father unable to cope with the loss had hung himself after shooting his wife in the head. They, remarkably, were soon forgotten. It is a fact that if something tragic happens and it leaves survivors behind the natural reaction is to sympathise, mourn, remember for a long time, but if there are no survivors (through whatever circumstances) the initial sympathy turns to wonder, and then forgetfulness. Why keep note of an event if there is no one left to remind you of it? A sad fact maybe but true.

It is this very fact that enabled the young Freud stein to come back to the castle a mere three years later. He had apparently come on in leaps and bounds and his attitude had changed and indeed his personality. His macabre interest in violence had disappeared and doctors thought he might have entered a phase, probably triggered by an early childhood event that had upset him and then lay hidden in the subconscious. At the age of nineteen, Eilrahc returned to his home and his doting parents and staff, seemingly a changed man.

But, inevitably, things began to happen. He frightened everyone he saw and seemed to have a hold on his mother. She always gave in to his every whim, while his father remained strict and always foreboding. He, therefore, held a deep hatred for Master Freud stein, some of it born out of jealousy as he would never become as powerful and feared as his father.

After the servants had finished for the evening, they left the Master's night-time drink on his table and retired to bed. At this moment, Eilrahc came into his own and proved not only how evil and calculating he is but also fairly intelligent. He had earlier mixed some poisonous mushrooms into a paste and swopped dishes with Alfrieda, the cook. The original apricot and mushroom soufflé was then vandalised. That night the Master would sample Eilrahc's amanita phalloids (more commonly known as the Destroying Angel). Once digested, these mushrooms would kill in minutes.

Emily Freud stein awoke in the early hours to find her beloved husband lying stiff, cold, and very, very dead. The shock of his untimely death brought on a sudden and fatal heart attack thus, transpiring an orphan, a rich, calculating orphan.

The police report was an accidental death, with no suspicious circumstances. The mushrooms were picked by mistake and Eilrahc made a big fuss blaming Stefan and all the rest of the staff. They were all instantly dismissed and told never to work again. They packed their belongings and moved out. After staying in rental accommodation they found themselves saved by the good heart of Emily Freud stein. She had left in her will the Old Coach House at the bottom of the cemetery to Stefan and his family for all of their loyal years' services.

Eilrahc had won by getting the servants out but they were still living on his land and with his late mother's permission. He put a stop to the gardener's work schedule, telling him to leave all land, after the orchard from the cemetery onwards. The old gentleman valued his job and so did everything he was told.

As time went on, the grass, weeds, and bushes, and trees grew in such an abundance that unless you knew the coach house was there it would never be visible. Stefan and his family lived quite comfortably and had little to do with Eilrahc. Life was liveable until boredom set in and Eilrahc decided he needed excitement. He needed to feel the power surging through him as the blood leaves the victim's body. He knew the castle grounds like the back of his hands so night-time escapades were no problem. He chose one of Stefan's family members, each month and kidnapped, assaulted, and then hid the body. He boxed cleverly with the police as no evidence of any foul play was found. He suggested to Stefan that the young girls, maybe, decided to move on somewhere else. After Terriane disappeared (the fourth girl) Stefan befriended a wolf and with his good sense of smell happened to come across an old well, hidden in the castle grounds where Terriane was found. She was naked, half-starved, suffering from pneumonia, and speechless with shock. They decided not to involve authorities but to sort it themselves.

They let Eilrahc know that they were going to get him and tricked him into going to the well. Stefan and the wolf attacked him and brought him to the ground. Stefan beat him about the face and head until he was unrecognisable, screaming in defeat and whimpering to be left alone. Stefan realised at the last minute how close he had come to almost ending another human's life. He didn't want to become like him and he told Eilrahc to leave the area in the next 24 hours or he would kill him. Eilrahc agreed and left the area.

Stefan stayed living in the coach house but maintained the castle on a daily basis. Eilrahc had definitely gone, no one had seen him for a while. Sometime later, two well-dressed gentlemen appeared and took purchase of the castle. They were happy for Stefan to keep the maintenance going while they were away on business and they were happy with the knowledge that the castle was looked after.

As time went by, locals became curious and decided to have a closer look. Word spread and out-of-state visitors appeared; young, old, all fascinated with the history and daring each other to enter the castle. This, of course, passed as fun for visitors and mild entertainment for Stefan and his family. The odd window got broke but Straker replaced it and always footed the bills. The problem came when these curious visitors left the castle in body bags. Word soon spread that Master Freud stein was back from the dead to avenge his death. This soon became the haunted castle. Lives were ended for no good reason and police had no clues to follow up. Eventually, the building was closed to the public and the grounds fenced off.

Nobody ever stayed at the castle again other than Johnson and Straker who passed through but never stayed the whole night. Nobody stayed until now.

Chapter Ten
Getting Closer

The fire had begun to glow a soft amber colour as the embers proceeded to cool. The wolf was gazing up at me and I caressed his head and planted a kiss between his eyes. I didn't know any of these people, yet, I felt so safe and relaxed amongst them. I looked around at everyone's faces and they returned my look. My eyes met the tall man's.

"Stefan, that's you, isn't it?"

He nodded slowly and meaningfully. I opened my mouth to say more and Stefan held up his hand and silenced me immediately.

"I know you have many, many questions and I will answer them all in good time but first we have work to do. We must save your friends from a fate surely worse than death."

My tears flowed freely as I spoke. "I know, two of my friends are gone, I just hope he didn't get them all."

Stefan gazed at me nodded his head and everyone got to their feet. "Eilrahc is back. We know this now."

I nodded and my fear grew another appendage. Stefan lifted his hands in the air and we all drew close just like the pied piper. I didn't know anyone's name but I felt a strange sense of family and unity. My hairy majestic friend never left my side. We all listened intently to the soft, hypnotic drawl of Stefan's voice.

"We go together, we stay together for protection and we fight together. The castle will be exorcised."

Daylight had begun to spread evenly over the surrounding area of woodland. We all followed Stefan silently and fearlessly into the daylight and onto the castle. We entered the building by the side door and strode purposely through the castle aware of every sound. The lower floor was empty. The cellar was also empty. I wanted to cry, I know I saw Liam's decapitated head, there on the floor. My friend as if sensing my distress, instantly brushed my side bringing me to my senses immediately. I knew whatever happened, I had to be strong.

We started to mount the stairs all in a single file, apart from my friend, who remained at my side. We all followed silently in Stefan's wake. As we walked along the landing, we passed the bathroom and the door was open. We walked past the carnage, every one of us seeing the carnage on the show but also letting it register somewhere in our subconscious to emerge later in a private moment of grief if we survived ourselves.

Eddie was sat on the toilet, completely naked and minus his penis. Dried blood had caked over his pubic hair and thighs and dripped on the carpet. Liam's body was hanging by his feet above the toilet. His back was to the door, scratches adjourned his back and a penis was shoved into his anus the wrong way in and a limp purple head with a pronounced slit gazed at us from the bloody orifice. Liam's head had been forced onto the hot tap, his tongue taken out, was lying on his head like a toupee.

Eventual foreclosure awaits every one of us. Eddie and Liam had already received their notice and I can only hope their suffering had been minimal. My notice was in the mail and I promised myself a sense of strength and courage to get by until the postman caught up with me. Despair is a foolish squandering of precious time.

We turned and surveyed each other, perhaps looking for an answer to all the tragedy and wondering what else awaited us. Everyone seemed to disperse and I hurried after them. Parting with a friend made me nervous even a newfound friend. Maybe I'm needy, neurotic, and paranoid, if not then obviously psychotic.

"Over here!" someone shouted. The room we had all avoided was the scene of the next victim, my Damon, my close companion. Always the boyish looks and charm, Eilrahc must have thought he was quite the catch. He looked quite respectable in comparison to Eddie and Liam. He was intact to start with and was sitting in a rocking chair with his legs crossed and his hands cupping his genitalia. It was obvious by the bloodstains on his upper thighs that Eilrahc had satisfied himself before strangling his conquest.

Stefan ushered us all into the corridor and dished out orders to small groups of us to spread out and search the upper floor. We were all to meet in the lounge downstairs as soon as our search was complete.

The wolf stayed by my side, all the time apart from when we reached the final bedroom. His pace quickened until my knees met his broad muscular torso as he barricaded the door. He let out a warning growl. I felt Stefan's warm breath on my ear and I instantly shrank back away from the door. Stefan opened it and there he was; the murderer, the rapist, the sick stupid son of a bitch. I felt the hate mount up inside and I wanted to rip the cock sucking mother fucker apart!

"Eilrahc, we meet again," Stefan spoke calmly.

Eilrahc giggled just like a small child. He was fat and ugly and wore a maniacal grin that just needed slapping.

I stepped forward and he stopped me by saying, "Charlie."

"We meet again and we will never be parted. You will carry on the family name, my Charlie," he gazed fondly at me. I fell to my knees in shock and Stefan steadied me.

"Explain yourself before I end your miserable life!" Stefan said calmly.

"The little whore's up the stick," giggled Eilrahc, "and she carries my offspring!"

That was the last thing I heard as my head hit the floor.

Chapter Eleven
The Beginning of the End

I came to in the lounge, lying on the sofa with the wolf at my feet. Stefan sat opposite in a high-backed chair and I suddenly noticed how old he had become. As I looked around the room, I saw Connie and Chris holding each other sobbing. I learned they had been bound and raped and that the three of us were impregnated with the bastard's sperm. We were destined to bear his offspring and to begin a new life with Stefan and his people. Our own lives were torn apart, our close friends crudely and shamelessly taken away from us. Our lives would never be the same again. No medical experts could restore our karma. We became the new generations of Stefan's family and one of our pleasures was to inflict pain and torture on this funny, grotesque shape that we kept locked in the cellar with only his giggles and half-eaten vermin as a company. Occasionally, he went walkabouts and again innocent lives were taken. The torn dismembered bodies filled out the cemetery and their existance stayed locked in our subconscious and the walls of the castle.

Innocence is pure and noble and needs to be kept safe and warm. Don't venture, lose the innocence, feel the pain.